All the Summer Voices

All the Summer Voices

Barbara Corcoran

Illustrated by Charles Robinson

Atheneum 1973 New York

Library of Congress catalog card number 73–76316
ISBN 0–689–30107–3
Published simultaneously in Canada by
McClelland & Stewart, Ltd.
Manufactured in the United States of America
by Halliday Lithograph Corporation
Designed by Nancy Gruber
First Edition

For Rosalie Gosbee Tinkham,
and for Roy Gosbee and his other children,
who reintroduced me to Essex.

And in memory of my grandparents, Harriet and
David Corcoran and my father, John Gilbert Corcoran,
who taught me to love Essex in the first place.

Acknowledgments:

In writing this book, I have found most helpful Dana Story's fine book about Essex, called *Frame Up*. I have also consulted Herbert A. Kenny's *Cape Ann: Cape America,* and a book published by the Junior League of Boston, *Along the Coast of Essex County;* a booklet compiled and written by Leslie Harris for the sesquicentennial committee, *150 Years a Town, Essex in Massachusetts;* also *Hamilton* by Daniel E. Safford; and *175th Anniversary, Town of Hamilton, Massachusetts,* the latter two given me by Harold A. Daley of the Hamilton Historical Society. The idea of the Model-T taxi came from a picture in *This Fabulous Century 1910–1920,* published by Time-Life Books.

I am also indebted to various people who helped me find material I needed, or who gave me invaluable information of their own, specifically: Mr. Melvin P. Jenkins; my cousin, Mrs. Ethel Towne; Mrs. Nancy Hubbard Wood; Mrs. Myra Taylor Cogswell; Mrs. Rosalie Gosbee Tinkham; Mrs. Stella Gosbee Migliori; Mr. Robert Robertson; Miss Pamela Bennett; and Mrs. Pauline Bennett. I thank them all.

It is almost impossible to write even a book of fiction about Essex without using the names that have pervaded her history since the beginning: Story, Burnham, Haskell, Andrews. But there is no character in my book that is intended to portray an actual person. Students of local history will discover that I did a little manipulating of actual events, like moving the icehouse fire ahead a few months, and blessing the town with the Model-T taxi; but on the whole I hope I have kept at least the spirit of the town as it was in those days.

All the Summer Voices

I

David leaned against the four-poster bed, trying to think of anything else he might need when he went to work in the shipyard tomorrow. He knew he'd be too sleepy to think straight when it was time to get up. It would be his first day as a regular hand; last summer he had just worked odd hours. He was looking forward to it, although he remembered how all his muscles had hurt for the first few days, muscles he didn't even know he had. He would be the youngest worker in the yard, and he grinned remembering how the men teased him, calling him "Half Pint" and sending him on crazy errands. This year he'd know better.

He checked his pants pockets to see if he had his knife and a handkerchief. And there was the withered little apple he'd picked up in the yard to give Lady before he left for work. That little horse really loved apples, even last year's.

He looked out the window to check the weather. The stars were bright, and there was a fresh breeze off the river.

Ought to be a good day. He noticed that Papa hadn't come home yet, and he frowned. Papa had been going down to Gloucester to the saloon a lot lately, and as usual David didn't understand why. Sometimes he'd go for months, even a year, without one single drink, and then there were the bad times when he'd come home unsteady on his feet, sarcastic to anybody except Mama, who tried to help him. Mama's face would get pale and tight with worry, but she never scolded Papa, and she never talked to David about the drinking, even when he had to help with getting him to bed. They both talked to Andrew as if he were another grown-up, but not to David.

He stared up at the sky, thinking about Andrew, only three years older and already gone, shipped out to the Banks with the Gloucester fleet. It was a hard, dangerous life, but David envied him just the same; he was free. Sometimes, though, when there was a storm, David would wake up in a cold sweat, worrying about Andrew, having dreamed that he was adrift alone in a dory off Sable Island or somewhere in a pea-soup fog with no provisions. Then he'd have to get up, even if it was a cold night, and kneel by the window, his elbows on the sill, taking deep breaths of the cold air and counting to one hundred. Then maybe he could get back to sleep. He told himself that Andrew had said he'd come back all right, and Andrew always did what he said he would.

"I'll be a real highliner," he'd said, "when I'm captain of my own vessel." A highliner, David knew, was the captain who brought back the biggest catch, and if Andrew said he could do it, he would. David wished he had his life as much under control as Andrew did. "Maybe you'll get a site on a vessel too, Davey, and after you learn the ropes, we'll have our own fleet. The O'Brien Brothers."

But David didn't want to go to sea. He didn't know what he wanted. I'm like Papa, he thought, but he didn't want to be. Papa had tried farming and couldn't make a go of it; once, when he was young, he'd shipped out on a whaler; he'd gone west to Colorado to mine for gold, but all he got was pneumonia; and he'd gone out with the fishing boats. But he got pneumonia again and almost died. And the doctor had said no more seagoing. "If Nathan O'Brien so much as sails past Ten Pound Island," he'd said, "I won't answer for him. His lungs are scarred up, Mrs. O'Brien. All scarred up."

So Papa had bought the secondhand carriage and an old circus horse with some money Grandpa loaned him and set up a taxi service, mostly taking people to and from the depot when the trains were due. It wasn't much of a living, and Papa didn't like being at everybody's beck and call, but he did it because he didn't know what else to do. And sometimes he drank too much, and that scared David more than anything.

David climbed into the featherbed, sinking down into its warm depths. Mama had put out a blanket for him, but you didn't need a blanket in June. He tried to figure out how much money he'd make this summer. Mama would need most of it, but she always saved out some for him. There would be the shipyard money and the street-light money. This would probably be the last summer for the street lamps; the town was beginning to replace the kerosene lamps with electricity. He wouldn't be sorry. He'd been lighting those darned lamps for almost five years now, ever since he was nine years old, and as long as he lived, he would never forget the cold winter nights, trying to get the lamps lit before the freezing wind off the marsh put out the flame, his arms cold and aching with the strain of holding the long pole steady. He was mighty glad Essex was getting electric lights.

He stiffened as he heard the back door open and close. He heard Mama's light, pleasant voice, and Papa's deep rumble. He listened for the signs, a stumble, a bump against a chair, a voice raised in annoyance. Nervous, he got up and went to the head of the steep stairs. The cathedral clock in the hall bonged the half-hour, and then he heard his father winding it, cussing when the key slipped out of his hand and clattered to the floor. Papa had had trouble with his right hand and arm ever since he'd gotten hurt a long time ago at the Giddings fire, but anyway the threads on the key were wearing down. He'd told Papa that, and that they could probably get another key made, but Papa was impatient with anything mechanical.

His father raised his voice and swore at the key now, kicking it across the floor. David heard it hit the baseboard. Mama said something in a low voice that David couldn't hear.

"You'd better help me up to bed," Papa said, his voice louder than normal. "I'm in that revolting condition again. That's what one of your church ladies told me. 'Mr. O'Brien,' she said, 'I beseech you, join the cold-water army.' " He laughed.

David came down the stairs. It made him furious that Papa should act like this and not even seem sorry. It was

humiliating to have a lady from the church talking to your father as if he were a common bum. "I'll help you upstairs, Papa," he said.

His father turned unsteadily and looked at him with a sardonic grin. "Ah, here is my helper. My dear son."

"Come on, Papa." He tried to get his father to lean on his shoulder.

"We're all right, Davey," Mama said. "You go back to bed."

"No, I'll help him up." David's voice was hard. Papa had no right to put Mama and him through this, time after time.

"Indeed, Mary," Papa said, "let my son do it. My son is a righteous young man, and it makes him feel good to help the weak and fallen."

"Nathan. . . ." Mama's voice held warning.

"My elder son, on the other hand, believes in live-and-let-live. He is not bowed down with moral scruples."

"Don't be cruel, Nathan." Mama's voice was sharp for the first time.

"No intention, no intention." He patted David's shoulder. "You go to bed, my boy. I can navigate the stairs."

"I'll help you, Papa."

Suddenly Papa was angry. "Damn it, I don't want to go to bed just now. Leave me alone."

David turned away, tears stinging his eyes. Although Mama called to him, he ran up the stairs to his room and shut the door. Let him fall up the stairs, then. Let him crash around and smash everything. Let him like Andrew better. The hell with him.

David pushed on the sash of the other little window, the one that stuck so often he usually didn't bother with it. With a great shove he got it up and put the stick under it to hold it open. He wanted all the fresh air he could get. He'd found a long time ago that when his temper made his head pound, the best thing was to take long, deep breaths of fresh air.

He could hear Mama and Papa talking, Papa quieter

now. After a long time David got into bed, but he couldn't sleep. He knew it wasn't right to get so mad at Papa; when he wasn't drinking, he was a good, kind father. But somebody had to try and stop him from drinking. He was endangering all of them. If he took to doing it all the time, pretty soon people wouldn't let their kids come to the house for Mama's music lessons, and Papa'd lose the taxi, and then what? Then they'd all be packed off to the Poor Farm, that's what would happen. Once, in anger, he had said this, and Papa had said, "Well, they got a nice view from the Poor Farm."

But it wasn't any joke. It could happen. With Andrew gone, David was the only one who could prevent it, and he wasn't sure he was up to it. Of course there was Grandpa, but Papa would never take any kind of gift from Mama's people, if he could help it.

Papa was so irresponsible about money. He'd had a job at the drugstore just last winter. Uncle Tom had gone to a lot of trouble to get it for him. But after a month he'd quit; said he didn't like standing around waiting for people to make up their minds between an orange phosphate and a Moxie. "A man has better things to do." And he'd gone off to the marsh to take pictures of birds with the Kodak that Grandpa gave him. But pictures of birds wouldn't buy groceries. If it hadn't been for Mama's pupils and the taxi money and David's lamplighting money, they'd have gone hungry. Or off to the Poor Farm.

David turned over restlessly. He wished he could figure Papa out. Last Easter when he'd made a little extra from selling the buggy, he took Mama to Boston to hear the *Mes-*

siah. And Mama was pleased! Sometimes when he thought about his parents, David felt as if he were trying to row upriver against the tide. They were like grown-up children.

Through the open windows he could hear voices drifting on the night air, boys wandering along the street, talking and laughing, one of them whistling. Voices in summer sounded different, carefree and easy. He sighed. He wondered if he'd ever be out there himself, strolling along the Causeway, laughing with the other fellows, maybe seeing a girl home. Or would he always be working and working to make ends meet, trying to keep Papa on the straight-and-narrow, taking care of Mama.

David was almost asleep when he heard Mama begin to play the piano softly, Papa's favorite song: "Believe Me If All Those Endearing Young Charms." Then they started singing together, quietly, and he felt so sad, he had to cover up his ears with the pillow so he couldn't hear them.

2

When David came into the kitchen for breakfast, Papa had already driven his passengers to the depot for the early train and had come home for a second cup of coffee. His long, narrow face looked haggard, and his pale blue eyes were bloodshot. He nodded to David, his manner a little constrained. When he had been drinking, he never referred to it afterward, but there was something that made it clear he was sorry.

" 'Morning, David," he said.

" 'Morning, Papa. 'Morning, Mama."

"Good morning, dear." His mother smiled at him. She was packing his dinner in the old lard pail. He lived near enough to come home at noon, but he liked to sit around the yard with the men, listening to the talk.

He pulled his chair up to the table, enjoying the warm feeling of the sun streaming in on his shoulders through the small-paned window.

"You got a hot day for your first day at the yard," Papa said. He stood up, tall and thin, his head almost touching the low ceiling. "You're going to work up a sweat, son."

"Better than rain," David said.

His father nodded. "Better than rain." He hunched his shoulders a little, as if remembering the cold rain that fell on him so often when he was driving the coach. He looked at his wife. "You got pupils today?"

He asked the question nearly every day, and if someone was coming for a piano lesson, he would often clear out of the house, as if he didn't know what to do with himself while the pupils were there. Sometimes he went down to Gloucester and had a few beers. Andrew said Papa felt bad because Mama earned more money than he did, but David wasn't sure if that was it or not.

"The Haskell twins are coming after school." Mama gave Papa an anxious glance to see how much he minded.

His mother looked pretty, David thought, with her cheeks pink from bending over the wood fire in the old range, and her brown hair, that she tried to keep combed back in a smooth knot, coming loose in little curls around her face. Mama was pretty for a woman her age.

Papa gave a scornful little laugh for the Haskell twins. "Da da da . . . da . . . da. . . ." He sounded the first notes of the scale, deliberately flatting. Mama laughed.

"I guess they'll never be concert pianists," she said, "but they work hard. Their mother sets great store by their learning to play."

"There's hardly a woman alive," Papa said, "who don't think her child is another Paderewski."

"Let us be grateful." Mama put a plate of bacon and eggs

in front of David. "Eat it all. You'll be hungry before noon."

Papa stood at the window, stooping a little to look out into the yard. "Lady's getting lame."

David looked up quickly. "Lame?"

"She's getting too old."

David felt a shiver go down his back. "She still acts young, Papa."

"Those circus people took a lot out of her. She's getting too old to work."

Carefully David cut up his eggs, fried hard the way he liked them. "I could take her down to Doc Fessenden's after work tonight and see what's wrong, why she acts lame."

"We've got no money for Doc Fessenden," his father said sharply.

David felt in his throat the hot anger that sometimes boiled up before he could stop it. "If we had the money that goes for. . . ." He stopped short at Mama's warning look. He had almost said "that goes for booze," and it scared him how close he had come to saying it.

His father gave him a long, hard look. "If that horse gets too old to work, she'll have to go down to Gloucester."

Going to Gloucester meant the glue factory. David put down his fork and knife.

"Eat your breakfast, Davey." Mama's voice held a sharp note of worry. "Your father's talking about someday—he's not talking about now. We'll all end up in the glue factory someday, for goodness' sake."

"I'm talking about now, if that horse is wore out." Papa left the room.

David clenched his teeth to keep his mouth from trembling. "He means it, Mama. He'd kill Lady for a little glue money."

"He's worried, that's all. Money is short. Eat your breakfast, Davey."

Andrew always said, Don't make Papa mad; he's a good man, but he's got a wicked temper. David knew that, all right; he was too big to get whacked with the razor strop now, but he wasn't too big to remember it. The trouble was, he had a temper himself. It made his blood boil for Papa to talk about getting rid of Lady as if she was some old, worn-out shoe. He found the money for booze, didn't he? You didn't get booze for nothing.

Before David left for work, he went out to the barn to see Lady. His father had unhitched her and left her to graze beside the barn. He'd thrown down the round, iron weight that held her by the bridle rein. She had her head down, munching grass, but she looked around when she heard David. A tuft of long grass hung from her mouth. Her eyes were bright and inquisitive as she came toward him, looking for whatever he'd brought her.

David laughed and gave her the wizened apple, stroking the white blaze on her brown forehead. He bent down and ran his hands over her legs. "Does it hurt, Lady? Are you getting rheumaticky or what? It's all those cold winter days you have to pull the sleigh out to the station in all that snow and everything. Anybody'd get stiff. But it's summer now; you'll be all right."

She nuzzled his hand and then his pockets, looking for more apples. Then, at his hand signal, she tossed up her head, reared up on her hind legs, crossed her front legs, and stood like that for a moment.

David clapped his hands, and she brought her feet down. "Good Lady. You're not old yet, not by a darned sight." He gave her a quick pat and ran down the road toward the Causeway. Lady didn't act old or sick. Anyway his father couldn't mean it, because without Lady he wouldn't be able to run the taxi.

In spite of his concern about Lady and his father and everything, David felt good. It was a sparkling morning with a light breeze coming off the river. He was going to work, and it felt fine. He stopped for a second or two to look into Chebacco Brook, where there had been a heavy run of alewives in the spring—fifty barrels caught in the nets, along with all the ones that made it upstream to the lake to spawn. His father had caught some, and they'd had alewives for dinner. David liked the taste of the little herrings but he was always a bit sorry when they got caught. They put up such a game fight to get up through the rapids to the lake. In the fall the young ones would come back to the deep saltwater for the winter, and then in the spring the whole thing would begin again, and people would come from miles around just to see the stream swarming with the little fish.

He hurried along, running at a jogging pace between the thin, steel streetcar tracks. Henry Peters went by, driving a load of hay. "Want a ride?" he yelled to David.

"Can't," David called back. "I'm going to work." He wished for a moment that he could. He loved to dig in under the load of hay, smelling that good smell, the dryness tickling his nose. But that was for little kids.

He came onto the Causeway, clomping his heels on the

board sidewalk. He waved to the oldest Knowlton boy, across the street on his way to the spar yard. Ahead of him the Berry boys were heading for the ropewalk. All along the street, men were turning off into the shipyards along the Causeway. There were vessels in all stages of building, some almost finished, some not yet framed up, some looking like the skeletons of huge fish. The beautiful little fishing schooner, the *Elsie,* had already been launched and people said she was to race the *Bluenose.* David wished he'd had a chance to work on her. He'd hung around the yard whenever he had the time, watching her being built.

The breeze off the marsh smelled of salt and fish, a smell David was so accustomed to, he hardly noticed it. A couple of clammers in high rubber boots were climbing into their dory, pushing off for the clam flats.

The big Paul Revere bell in the Congregational Church rang out the hour for work, and David ran across the street to the yard. The men were putting down their dinner pails, taking off sweaters, getting tools ready. Two men began to saw a fifty-foot plank. Thc whine of the saw and the smell of sawdust filled the morning air.

On one of the schooners, the dubbers were working, trimming the frame with adzes. The plankers would follow, laying on the heavy oak planks. One strip of plank around a boat's hull was called a "streak." David watched them a moment while he waited for the owner, who was looking at the plans the loftsman had brought down to him from the mold-loft. He'd watched this team of dubbers and plankers before, and he knew they were so good that sometimes they could get two streaks done in a day.

The pinging sound of the caulkers' mallets striking iron rang out over the sounds of broadax, whipsaw, and adze. The caulkers, who were working on a different vessel, traveled from yard to yard, as they were needed. Sometimes they were a tough lot, but David loved to watch them work with their assortment of tools: dumb irons, hawsing irons, T-shaped wooden mallets made of mesquite or live oak, with foot-long handles. Part of their job was to fill the seams and joints with oakum and cotton.

One of the joiners, a man named Pete Alzar, waved to David. Everybody said Pete was such a skilled workman, he could make a concert violin with just his adze and his broadax, if he took a mind to.

Another carpenter, Tom Doyle, looked up from the frame he was working on. "Hey, Davey, bring me a bucket of nails."

Horace Wesley stopped sawing long enough to yell, "Hey, Half Pint, bring me a forty-foot spar!"

"Davey!" yelled Henry Hubbard, who was boring holes for the fasteners, with his long auger, "bring me a bottle of rum!"

"Davey, get me. . . ."

"Hey there, Half Pint, get the lead out!"

David laughed. He was back at work, all right.

3

David was on the run all morning, helping unload the lumber that Bus Merrill brought up with his big black horse, getting tools and material the men needed, and once in a while being allowed to drive a few nails, under the watchful supervision of one of the men. He was careful with tools, and although they grumbled at him, they never had to undo anything he did.

Toward noon the breeze died down and the sun was hot. David pushed his cloth cap back from his sweaty forehead and wiped his face with his sleeve. His muscles trembled. He tried to pretend he wasn't tired, but when the foreman told him to take a couple of minutes off, he sank down gratefully on a pile of lumber.

Pete Alzar sat beside him, stretching his long, thin legs in front of him. "Tired, Davey?"

"No. I'm fine."

Horace Wesley came over and planted his wide feet in

front of them. "Now if this was the good old days, we'd be gettin' our morning cup of grog."

"It wasn't a cup," Pete said. "It was just a tot of rum."

"Morning and afternoon," Horace said. "And welcome, I'll be bound."

One of the caulkers joined the conversation. "Davey here'd be too young to get his. He'd have to take it home to his pa."

Pete Alzar gave the caulker an angry stare.

David felt the hot rush of blood in his face. Everybody knew about Papa; everybody thought it was funny that he drank more than was good for him. Nobody respected a man who drank. They talked about Papa as if he was some common, falling-down, town drunk. He got up and walked away quickly, to a shady place under the prow of the vessel that was almost finished. He could smell the tar from the oakum. Warren Larimer, one of the outside joiners, was leaning against the staging, sorting out his hand-planers and scrapers. He was one of the outside team that came in to plane the planks lengthwise and crosswise, "traversing" and finally hand-scraping them till they shone like satin.

"How you doin', Davey?" Warren said. He was a young, sandy-haired man, and David admired him because he was the star pitcher on the town ball team.

"All right." David still felt stung by the caulker's taunt. It was hard to talk.

"Guess they ain't ready for the finish men here yet," Warren said, running his hand over the planks. He sauntered off.

Horace Wesley and Harry Duke came over to David.

"Tom was only fooling, Davey."

"I don't care." David looked away.

Horace put out his big hand and tugged at David's cap. "Harry, you ever see a boy with such a dirty face? Before you go home tonight, Davey boy, you better stick that head of yours under the pump or your ma'll think you turned into a Portygee." He grinned at Harry. "You ever see such a dirty face?"

"Never did," Harry said. "You'd think he'd done a little work around here instead of lollygagging around like some girl at a tea party."

David tried to smile. He knew they were jollying him, trying to cheer him up. Last year when the men teased him, it had made him nervous because he couldn't tell whether they meant it or not, but one morning the foreman had said, "Don't pay them any mind, David. They wouldn't take out after you if they didn't like you." So he had learned to enjoy it, though he never could think of anything funny to say back to them.

The rest of the morning went quickly, and he was surprised when the Congregational bell pealed out the signal for dinner. Some of the men went home, but some, like David, had brought their pails. They clustered under the shadow of the boats to eat and talk. David liked to listen to them, especially to the tall tales of the sea that Ben Platt spun, and the stories of life in the yards thirty or forty years ago that old Mr. Reuben told.

When he'd finished eating, he walked out on Corporation Wharf to stretch his legs. Over at the James yard they were building a whaler. Whaling sounded exciting, but his father said it wasn't, except for the short time when they were actually catching a whale. Papa had shipped out on a whaler once, while he was still in his early years, and he said you nearly went crazy with boredom and homesickness.

David stopped beside the road to wave to the driver of a wagonload of dories. The big platform on wheels, which came from Amesbury on its way to Gloucester, was loaded with half-a-dozen dories, each one painted and named to the order of the buyer. Two small black horses pulled the load. Today they were streaked with sweat, and one of them limped a little. David thought of Lady, hoped she was all right. He watched the load of dories go down the Causeway.

Back at work, the foreman asked him if he'd take one end of the big saw. The man who usually did it had gone home with an attack of asthma. "Think you can handle it, Davey?"

"Sure," Davey said, though he was far from sure. He seized his end, as Terry Testa laid the long plank over a wooden support.

Terry's olive-skinned face peered at him. "Don't worry, Davey. I make it easy on you."

But sawing these big planks wasn't easy. In a few minutes David's arms ached as if they were being raked with fire, and he was coughing from the cloud of sawdust they raised. He stuck with it, though, until midafternoon, when the foreman came over and looked at the job they'd done.

"That's enough for today. You did a good job, Davey." And for the rest of the afternoon, until the bell rang four-o'clock quitting time, he gave David easy jobs. "You done a good day's work, Davey."

David was pleased but he was almost too tired to think about it. He gathered up his sweater and dinner pail and started home. Mr. Tarr's auto passed him. David watched it chugging over the gravel road. He hadn't seen many cars, and they fascinated him. He wished he could open up the hood and see what the engine was like. Mr. Tarr's was a Maxwell, a high machine with a short wheelbase; it looked like a buggy, only without a top.

Mr. Tarr waved and honked his horn. It sounded like

"Ra-roó-ra," a nice jaunty kind of a sound. David watched him until he was out of sight and only a thin cloud of dust and a smell of gasoline were left.

He walked home much more slowly than he had walked to work. If I had an auto, he thought, I'd be home in a minute. Some day I'm going to get me one of them. Maybe if he worked hard at the shipyard and got to be a good builder, he could get an auto. He doubted it though. Autos cost an awful lot, and the men who worked in the yards didn't make much. Papa said boat building was on the skids anyway; there hadn't been nearly as many boats built this year as last. Some people said now the Essex Boat Club was going great guns, there'd be a boom in pleasure boats, but David didn't know. All he knew was, some way or other he wanted to get ahead. He didn't want to be worrying all the time about money, the way his father did, or running around when other folks called him. He wouldn't like that any better than Papa did. He wished he could get a college education, like his grandfather.

Pretty soon he'd go up to Hamilton and have a talk with his grandfather. Grandpa always had a lot of ideas. But of course he couldn't even think about college, when Papa couldn't even make ends meet.

He came into his yard, swinging his empty pail, thinking about the good hot supper Mama would have for him. She'd make him clean up first and then she'd feed him good, and he'd go to bed early. He was really tired.

He walked around the corner of the house to the back door and stopped short. The coach that his father used for the taxi still sat in the yard near the barn, and Lady was quietly munching grass. Papa should have been on his way to meet the train before now, but he was nowhere in sight.

David ran to the back door and opened it. From the front of the house he could hear somebody playing "Brahms' Lullaby" very slowly, counting out "One-and-Two-and . . ." hitting wrong notes every bar or two. His mother came into the kitchen, looking worried.

"Where's Papa?"

She shook her head. "He went out when Mary came for her lesson. I haven't seen him since. I thought maybe you were Papa. . . ."

Angrily David said, "He's going to miss his passengers."

His mother looked out the window. "He'll be along in a minute."

"You know he won't." David felt sick with anger and resentment. How could his father act this way? "You know darned well he won't. I'll have to go out to the station."

She looked at him doubtfully. "You must be so tired. . . ."

"Yes, I'm tired," he said furiously. "I'm a darned sight tireder than Papa is. I've done a hard day's work. But somebody has to go get those people."

Her mouth trembled but she frowned at him. "Don't speak like that about your father."

"My father. . . ." He broke off in disgust, and turned away.

"Wash your face, David," she called after him. "Wash up first."

"There isn't time," he said. He was already hitching Lady to the coach. It was true, there wasn't time, but also he was angry enough to hope the passengers would notice how he came to his father's rescue, David who'd been working like a man all day in the yard. "Go, Lady," he said, climbing up onto the high driver's seat. "Git. We're late." He didn't look back at his mother, but he knew she was standing in the doorway watching him. She always stuck up for Papa, every time.

He urged Lady along at a fast trot, but before they got to the station, he slowed her down. She really was limping a little. Maybe it was just a stone caught in her shoe. He'd look at it later.

They were late. The half-dozen men who had come in on the train from Boston were looking impatient. The trainmen had the engine on the turntable and were turning it around, getting it ready for the trip back in the morning.

"Well, Davey," Mr. Milliken said, heaving his two-hundred-and-some pounds into the coach. "We thought you'd forgot us."

David forced a smile. "No, sir. Sorry to keep you waiting."

The other passengers clambered aboard, all of them giving him a friendly greeting except old Mr. Ryan, who never gave anybody the time of day. He grumbled and mumbled as he swung himself stiff-legged into the coach.

"Looks like you've been making mudpies, Davey," Mr. Billings said. The other men, except Mr. Ryan, laughed.

"I just got in from work," David said. "Didn't have time to wash up."

"We don't care," Mr. Luscomb said, "just so you get us home. It was hot and dirty in Boston today, mighty hot and dirty. I'm going to bundle up my wife and kids and take 'em off to Wingarsheek Beach for a picnic, so I can get in a good swim."

David turned Lady around and started the long trip back, going up one road after another to leave his passengers at their homes. After the first few minutes they stopped talking to him and just talked to each other. The stock market. Politics. David only half-listened. Then Mr. Milliken began telling about a suffragette he'd listened to on Boston Common during his lunch hour.

"Pretty as a picture," he said. "Looked like Alice Roosevelt. There she was, up on that soapbox, spieling away about women's rights. She drew quite a crowd."

"How'd it come out, Harvey?" Mr. Billings said. "She make any converts?"

"Well, no. Trouble was, she got so het up, she fell off that durned soapbox."

The men laughed, and David grinned, although he was secretly in favor of the suffragettes. His mother would have liked to be one if she had had the time.

"Well, they don't know when they're well off," Mr. Luscomb said. "Those little ladies just don't know when they're well off."

"I was looking at a new Locomobile today," Mr. Anson said. He was the youngest of the men, and the most stylish, with his Arrow shirts and his suits with matching vests that he wore even in the summertime.

"That'll run a man around three, four thousand dollars," Mr. Luscomb said. "That's a lot of money, George."

"The one I want is the 40 model, runs around four thousand five-hundred," Mr. Anson said.

Mr. Ryan said the first words he'd uttered since he got into the coach. "Fools and their money are soon parted."

George Anson sounded annoyed. "Oh, come on, Wilbur. A man has to keep up with the times."

"I don't," Mr. Ryan said.

"If you're thinking along those lines, George," Mr. Milliken said, "what you want is the Peerless. They've got a real swell auto."

David stopped Lady in front of Mr. Anson's house and waited while Mr. Anson climbed over the others and got out.

"No," Mr. Anson was saying, "it comes down to the Locomobile or the new Pierce Arrow." He paid David and waved to the others. "See you fellows in the morning."

David turned Lady around, and she clopped back down the street. He was enjoying the conversation about autos; he was very much interested in them.

"George really going to get a machine, you think?" Mr. Luscomb asked.

"Oh, you know George. He's full of hot air."

"The man's a fool," said Mr. Ryan. "Born a fool and he'll die a fool."

Mr. Milliken chuckled. "Lawrence, you're awful hard on a young man."

"No need to be a fool because he's young," Mr. Ryan said. As David pulled up in front of his house, Mr. Ryan got his leather valise and his gold-headed cane and climbed laboriously out of the high coach. He paid David and nodded curtly.

The conversation went back to money, the high cost of living, problems in stocks and bonds, and David stopped listening.

Mr. Milliken, who was the last one to get out, tossed a magazine on the seat beside David. "Picked it up for my Tod, but he hasn't read the last one I got him. You keep it, Davey."

It was the newest book about Frank Merriwell's adventures. "Thank you, Mr. Milliken."

On the way home he thought about which of those men he'd like to be like. Mr. Milliken was the nicest, though Mr. Luscomb was nice, too. He agreed with Mr. Ryan about Mr. Anson. It would be fine to have a new Locomobile, but Mr. Anson had five kids, and everybody said Mrs. Anson worked like a horse trying to keep the whole bunch going.

It occurred to him that not one of them had asked where his father was. Bitterly, he thought, "They knew." He felt ashamed. Respectable people didn't drink; everybody knew that. You'd never catch any of those men hanging around a saloon. That was why Essex was a dry town; that showed you what Essex people thought of folks who drank. Bums. People said Mrs. Pettigrew drank, but if she did, she did it on the quiet, in her own bedroom, and anyway people felt sorry for her because her little boy had drowned in the river. That was a different situation altogether.

As David let Lady's reins go slack, letting her turn into the yard, his father came out of the house. Without looking at him directly, David saw that he walked steadily, but his face was flushed. David jumped down and began to unhitch Lady.

"There was no need your going," Papa said. "I got home right after you left."

"Oh. Well, I thought. . . ."

His father interrupted him. "I know good and well what you thought, and I get sick and tired of what you think."

David felt his own anger rising. How could Papa talk that way, when he'd been trying to help. "Somebody had to meet the train. . ."

"Meeting the train is my job," his father said coldly. "I don't need any help."

"Sometimes you do." David knew he should stop talking. He'd regret it if he talked back. But he said, "Sometimes you've missed it."

"And if I do, that's my affair, not yours. When I want you to take care of my business, I'll tell you. I'm not a child or a half-wit. I'm quite capable of managing my own life. Is that clear?"

"Yes," David muttered.

After his father went into the house, David fed and watered Lady, trying to keep back the angry tears. He threw himself down in the haymow, which his father hated to have him do because it ruined the hay.

He didn't answer when his mother called him. Finally he went out to the pump and washed his face. He took the long pole to light the lamps, and then he went back and got the ladder. Might as well let people know there was one O'Brien who could do his job right.

At each lamp post he propped the ladder up and climbed up to clean the glass lamps till they shone. Then he filled the lamps with enough oil to burn till about nine o'clock. The town selectmen had ruled that that was enough. If anybody was out after nine, he was probably up to no good, they said, and he could just get along without the lamplight. Up to no good. Papa was often out after nine o'clock, though he didn't hang around Essex much. Nothing to do in Essex at night, he always said. David polished the last lamp. That was just it—that's what Papa didn't seem to understand; a man wasn't supposed to be looking for things to do at that time of night. Especially a married man with a family.

He should be home where he belonged, keeping out of trouble. Most men were in bed and asleep by nine o'clock, and up by five or six. Papa said he couldn't sleep, but David thought he just didn't try. Anybody could sleep if he had a mind to.

He hoisted the short ladder over his shoulder and started home. Instead of cooling off his anger, he had worked himself up even more. He wondered if Papa would be gone again tonight. No wonder Lady had a lame leg, having to haul Papa off to Gloucester or Ipswich or Beverly all the time so he could get a drink and hang around with bums.

He looked up the street before he turned off toward his own yard, half-expecting to see Old Man Jasper, the town drunk, shuffling along, talking to himself. People laughed at him, and kids teased him, but whenever David saw him, he felt sick. That was how a man who drank could end up.

His mother was sitting in the kitchen working on a piece of music. Through the parlor door he could see Papa reading the paper by the kerosene lamp. Papa didn't look up, and David avoided looking at this mother.

"You must be hungry." She put a plate of food in front of him and for a moment she rested her hand on his shoulder.

After he had eaten, he went to bed and pulled the quilt over his head. He wondered if the whole summer was going to be like this.

4

On Saturday it rained. The inboard joiners started the cabinetwork inside the *Mildred W.*, the schooner that would soon be ready for launching. And the fo'c'sle men worked on the bunks and the galley. When the rain increased to a drenching downpour, the carpenters worked in their shop.

"Why don't you go over to the oakum loft, Davey," the foreman said. "Learn how they spin oakum."

David liked the oakum loft, although he was never quite at ease around the tough caulkers. He went up the steps, wiping the rain from his face with his cap. The stove, set in sand at the far end of the room, was roaring, and already the room was hot and smoky. There were windows on the river side. The other walls were filled with pictures of schooners, and fierce photographs of prize fighters aiming a punch toward the camera. The men sat on kegs, with slanted boards behind them to rest their backs.

There were five caulkers in the room, two of them working, just then. They wore a leather apron over one knee, working with a ball of oakum on the floor. They pulled out the strands, stretching and rolling them between their hands, spinning and winding the strands into smaller balls that they would be able to work with.

David blinked in the blue haze of smoke and watched. The oldest man, Billy Ipswich, nodded to him. Billy's real name was Haskell, but he had moved to Essex from Ipswich ten years ago, and since there were already several Billy Haskells, he was nicknamed Billy Ipswich.

"Sit down over here next to me," Billy Ipswich said. "You know how to spin?"

"No," David said, "but I've watched a couple of times."

Johnny Harris laughed and spit an arc of tobacco juice toward the corner. "Watchin' ain't doin', Mister."

David watched Johnny pull the strands of hemp over his knee as he worked. He didn't think winding it into balls would be too different from helping his mother wind her skeins of yarn.

The caulkers paid no attention to him. They talked and laughed a good deal, and the smell of pipe smoke and the wood stove and the tar from the hemp seemed to fill the room like something solid enough to touch. But David liked being there. He listened to everything the men said, thinking now and then how shocked his mother would be if she heard some of the caulkers' stories. But if you were going to be a man and work with men, you had to get used to that kind of talk. His father had spoken to him about it last year, when he first went to work in the yard. "You don't have to use it," he'd said. "But you might as well get used to hearing it, because that's the way a lot of men talk." He'd never heard his father talk like that, but maybe he did when he was alone with the men.

David looked at the silvery streaks of rain on the windows and thought about Lady. She'd seemed pretty good all week, and Papa hadn't said anything more about getting rid of her, but this rain wouldn't help her any.

"Hey, Mister!" Johnny suddenly barked at him. He tossed a ball of oakum at David.

Startled, David dropped it. The men roared with laughter.

"Johnny, you scared that little boy half to death," Al Silva said. Al, who came from Beverly but worked now in Essex, was an Italian with a long scar on his cheek. Because of the scar, David thought he must be a dangerous character, and he tried to avoid him.

"Mister," Johnny said to David, "your old man goin' out to the depot in all this rain to pick up them gentlemen on the train?"

"I guess so," David said.

"I guess so." Johnny mimicked him, making his voice higher than David's. "If it was me, I'd let them high muck-a-mucks stand out there in the rain and catch p-noo-monia, before I'd go after 'em."

"If they wasn't such a lazy bunch of bastards, they could walk home," Billy Ipswich said. "Them bankers and brokers, sittin' on their asses up there in Boston, messin' around with our hard-earned money. . . ." He spat a stream of tobacco juice across the room.

"They don't mess with your money, Billy," Tom Peters

said. "Your money don't never get out of that Ipswich saloon."

"That's where I ought to be right now," Billy Ipswich said. "Having a pint."

"If it was me," Pete DuBois said, "if it was me run that taxi, I'd leave 'em out there on a day like this, and I'd comfort myself at the saloon."

Johnny laughed. "Ten'll get you one that's what old Nathan O'Brien is doin' right this minute. That man, he knows how to tuck it away."

They all looked at him, and David felt himself grow stiff. They were challenging him. Would he defend his father? He looked Johnny in the eye. "My father has a lot of pain," he said, his voice sounding loud in his ears. "He hurt his arm real bad in the Giddings fire. . . ." Their scornful laughter stopped him. He felt the heat of his anger turning his face red.

"Boy," Johnny said, "that Giddings fire, that was so long ago, my grandpa hardly remembers it."

David stood up. "A man can get hurt for life," he said. "It makes his arm feel better when he drinks a little." His own words surprised him because he had never thought of that reason for his father's drinking. Andrew must have said it a long time ago, and it had stuck in the back of his mind.

Over the mocking laughter of the others, Al Silva's voice rose. "Let the kid alone. He's sticking up for his pa. Let him alone."

As quickly as it had started, the teasing stopped. Billy Ipswich began a long story about a girl he'd met in Newburyport.

"Sit down, Davey," Al Silva said. "Cool off."

David sat down, his head still pounding. His feelings were confused, but it seemed to him that somehow he had come out all right in whatever test it was they had put him to. Thanks to Al Silva, of all people, he had come out all right.

At dinner time David went outside. It was still raining, but he had to get a little fresh air. He went over to the *Mildred W.* and found a dry place under the stern. He had just bitten into an egg sandwich when Al Silva came up to him and squatted down beside him. For a few minutes he didn't say anything; he just opened his dinner pail, took out a big chunk of salami and a bottle of red wine, and gave them his whole attention. David felt nervous, not knowing what to say.

"How's your pa?" Al said finally. "Ain't seen him in a dog's age."

"He's all right," David said.

Al nodded and chewed on his meat, staring with narrowed eyes against the rain. He took a long drink from his wine bottle. "I remember a time, I wasn't a whole lot older than you, I come down here lookin' for a job." He tipped the bottle again. His Adam's apple moved up and down as he drank. "Got one. First payday, I went down to Gloucester and got drunk." Still staring out at the rain-streaked river, as if he saw something out there, he laughed. "Picked a fight with this big feller from Rockport. He was in a fair way to beat my brains out, and everybody sittin' there watchin'." He laughed again. "Your pa come over and says, 'Leave the boy be. Leave thc boy be,' he says. Now your pa's a tall man but he's skinny. This son-of-a-seacook from Rockport that's beatin' on me, he'd make four of your pa. But you know what happened?"

"What?" David had stopped eating and was listening intently. It seemed important.

"Well, this son-of-a-seacook from Rockport, he takes one good look at your pa, and what does he see there, in your pa's eye? I dunno what he saw. Plenty of nerve, I guess. A man that means what he says, that ain't scared of nobody." He wiped his mouth and shook his head. "That son-of-a-seacook from Rockport, he just walked outa that saloon without one more word. And your pa looks at me, and he says, 'You better get on home, son. You're a mess.' " He chuckled. "He was right. I was a mess. And I got on home." He stood up, still looking out into the rain. Then he walked away without another word, without even looking at David.

David sat for a long time without eating, thinking about what Al had told him, trying to picture the scene. Papa would have been maybe ten years younger then. But David knew what that look was, that had turned away the son-of-a-seacook from Rockport. Papa wasn't scared of anybody. David finished his lunch and went back to the oakum loft, whistling.

5

David went to church Sunday morning because he liked to listen to the music. His mother played the organ and directed the choir, and the music was nice. Papa never went.

On this Sunday, at the end of David's first working week in the yard, Papa picked them up in the buggy after church and they drove out to the cemetery. It was the anniversary of Grandfather O'Brien's death, the fifteenth anniversary; he had died before David was born. Grandfather O'Brien was a Civil War Navy hero. He had been the medical officer on Admiral Farragut's flagship at the time of the battle in Mobile Bay. David knew the whole story—he'd been brought up on it. He knew, as vividly as if he'd been there himself, how Admiral Farragut had had himself lashed to the mast so he could direct the battle. David could almost smell the roaring fire, feel the shattering blows, as ship rammed into ship. Grandfather O'Brien had been badly wounded, and years later he had died of those wounds. He'd been decorated; he was a hero. Now on his grave there was a black iron cross, and on the granite monument the inscription read: Capt. Timothy O'Brien, U.S. Navy, fought in the War Between the States. Born 1839, Died 1895. Rest In Peace. Beside the gray monument were two small white headstones. One gave the name and dates of his grandmother. The other read: Nathan O'Brien—Born 1871—Died—

Once David had said to his mother that he was proud of his hero grandfather, and she said sharply, "You'd do better to spend your time being proud of your father. There's more than one way to be a hero." He hadn't known what she meant, but now, looking at that small headstone with the date of death still blank, he thought of what Al Silva had told him and he felt a sharp pain in his ribs. God, he said in his mind, don't let Papa die.

But his father rose from putting flowers in front of Grandfather's grave and said calmly, "All right. Time to go." And there was no sign of mortality hanging around him.

"I wonder if Tom and Eloise will come," David's mother said on the way home. "I cooked up a big fish chowder, just in case."

Papa shrugged. "You never know. No sense wasting food when you don't know."

"It won't be wasted. We'll eat it." She took the pins out of her Sunday hat with the velvet flowers on it, and held it in her lap, as Lady jogged along the gravel road pulling the buggy.

Papa pointed the whip handle toward the horse. "See how

she limps in that front foot?"

"Well, she's not as young as she used to be," Mama said comfortably. "None of us are."

"But the rest of us don't have to pull that coach," Papa said. "I'd be in a pretty pickle if she give out on me, halfway home from the station."

"She won't give out, Papa," David said anxiously.

His father looked at him. "She won't, eh? You got that word from on high? You pick up that news in church?"

"Nathan," Mama said. "Don't be sacrilegious."

"The boy's got to learn," Papa said, "that wishing don't make it so."

Mama sighed. "What a shame."

Uncle Tom and Aunt Eloise hadn't showed up by dinner time so they ate without them. Sometimes they came over from Topsfield to put flowers on Grandfather's grave, and sometimes they didn't. Uncle Tom owned a drugstore over there and he made a good deal of money. They lived in a big Victorian house with six bedrooms.

"All those rooms," Mama often said, "and no children to fill them up. What a pity."

But David thought they were glad they had no children. On the few occasions when he and Andrew had stayed there overnight, he knew it made Aunt Eloise very nervous. She kept picking up after them, and straightening out, and saying, "Oh, boys! do be careful!" The house was full of breakable things, all of them expensive. David didn't like to go there. Neither did Papa. Uncle Tom always gave him advice about how to make money, how to save, and all that. And afterward Papa would say bitterly to Mama,

"Tom never did figure out that a man can't save money if he ain't got any." David thought Uncle Tom looked down on Papa.

Today after dinner, when he'd filled the coal hod for Mama and brought in the kindling, David went out and got Lady and took her out back of the barn, where the grass was green. He lay on his stomach on the horse's back, his head on his arms, enjoying the warmth of the sun and the laziness of the afternoon. Up against the back of the barn, the sleigh and the big pung were covered with tarpaulin, making them look like big black animals. For a moment David thought of winter, some of it bad, with the icy wind cutting through him, and the snow blowing in wet and cold off the ocean, but a lot of it nice too, like skating, and riding on Grandpa Andrews' iceboat up at Chebacco Lake, and hooking pungs. His mother hated to have him hook pungs—she was afraid he'd get his foot caught under the heavy runners of those big sleighs, but it was Papa who taught him how to do it safely. David and his friend Chet would sometimes hook pungs all over the North Shore, as far away as Beverly Farms or Manchester, and sometimes the men who drove the pungs wouldn't even know they were there, hanging on for dear life to the back, crouching down out of sight when the driver turned around.

But he was glad it was summer now. He'd brought home his first pay envelope last night. Mama had put it in the Sandwich glass milk pitcher, at the back of the cupboard.

"When I get enough," David said, into one of Lady's ears, "I'm going to get some liniment for your leg. Grandpa Andrews uses liniment for his rheumatism, and it makes him feel a whole lot better." He would have to ask at the drugstore how much horse liniment was.

At the sound of his voice Lady threw up her head and turned to look at him with her dark, soulful eyes. Then she reared up daintily, pawing the air with her front feet, and David slid off that comfortable, sweaty back into the grass. He rolled over, sneezing from a noseful of timothy grass, and got to his feet, laughing. Lady hadn't pulled that trick in a long time. He rubbed her nose, and put his cheek against the black velvet. "You could still be a good circus horse, I bet. You're full of tricks, like a darned little colt." He smoothed back her flanks. "Don't you worry, Lady, nothing bad is ever going to happen to you as long as I'm around."

She nickered and nipped at his ear.

"Listen, I'm going for a swim. See you later." Maybe he could find Chet or Pete or some of the other guys, and go diving off the bridge.

Later, when he came back from the river, wet and shivering, there was an automobile in the yard. He could hardly believe it. Then he realized whose it must be: Uncle Tom's. He'd been talking about getting one for a long time. Although his teeth were chattering with cold, David stopped to inspect the machine. Even before he read the name on the radiator, he knew it was a Ford. He'd read about Henry Ford's autos, and seen pictures of them. He was excited about seeing a real one.

He walked all around it, admiring its wooden frame, its top, its height. It *looked* like an automobile, not like a buggy with no horse. It was around seven feet tall and it looked like some kind of big bug, with those headlamps that made eyes on the front. David touched the shiny black upholstery and then looked guiltily toward the house; his wet fingers had left a thin mark. He rubbed it out with his fist. Aunt Eloise would hit the roof if he got marks on it.

He peered at the radiator grill and inspected the carriage lamps on the sides and marveled at the running boards. He wished he could see the engine. Maybe he'd get a chance later because Uncle Tom would certainly want to show it off. He went in the kitchen door.

6

Uncle Tom wiped his mouth carefully with one of Mama's good linen napkins. "Mary," he said, "I was saying to Eloise only this morning, 'nobody,' I said, 'nobody makes a fish chowder like Mary.' "

Mama smiled. "Thank you, Tom. I always think of you when I make it." Then as if she had caught the glint of amusement in Papa's eyes, she added, "Because I know you're partial to it."

"He's just plain partial to food," Aunt Eloise said. "He's getting fat." She leaned over and poked Uncle Tom's stomach. He frowned and pulled it in.

"A man broadens out a little as he gets older," he said.

"Look at your brother," Aunt Eloise said. "Not an ounce of fat on him."

Uncle Tom changed the subject. "You like my auto, do you, Davey?"

"Oh, you bet," David said. "I've read a lot about those Fords, but I haven't seen one before."

"They're the coming thing," Uncle Tom said. "That feller over in Michigan, that Henry Ford, he's caught onto this idea of making a whole bunch of cars at one time, all of 'em alike. Cuts down the overhead. It'll revolutionize the country."

"Lady and I had to pull one out of the mud over to Gloucester last month," Papa said.

"Feller didn't know how to drive. Shouldn't try to go through deep mud like some kind of clam digger. Got to use common sense." As they got up from the supper table, he said, "Nathan, speaking of that horse of yours, I got a proposition for you."

Papa looked wary. Uncle Tom was always full of propositions, some good, some not so good, though he himself always seemed to prosper. "What kind of a proposition?" Papa said.

In the sitting room Uncle Tom sat down carefully on the horsehair sofa, spreading his coattails out around him like a fan. "Got a proposition to make us both some money, and make life a whole lot easier for you."

"Fire away," Papa said.

Mama and Aunt Eloise were clearing away the dishes, and David sat on the little wooden footstool near the door, hoping no one would notice him and think of something for him to do. He wanted to hear Uncle Tom's proposition.

Uncle Tom took his gold watch out of his vest pocket and looked at it, held it to his ear, wound it, put it back in his pocket before he answered.

"Well, sir," Uncle Tom said, "I'll tell you what I got in mind." He pulled his chin up and straightened his tie, which was already straight. "Feller I know over to Rowley had a little, no'account farm, mostly rocks, but this chap is crazy wild about autos. Buys 'em secondhand, mind you, and fools around with 'em till he gets 'em running. Well, this man is into me for a lot of money. His wife was real sick here a while back, and he had to buy all kinds of medicine and stuff. She's better now, but he hasn't got a dime. All went to the doctor and the hospital, to hear him tell it. I finally lost my patience over this whopping big bill he owes me, and I told him I'd have to sue."

Papa, leaning one elbow on the fireplace, looked down at his brother and frowned. "How could you sue a man who was in a lot of trouble like that?"

Uncle Tom gave him a long, exasperated look. "Nathan, you got no business sense."

"Thank God, then," Papa said.

"The way you look at things is all wrong. The world won't run on sympathy. Believe me. I'm a kindly man, but I have to get paid or I go out of business."

Papa shook his head impatiently. "We've been through this before."

"Sure as shooting, we have. And I tell you again, Nathan, it's your attitude makes you poor as Job's turkey. If you was a practical man, you'd have a bundle by now. You're a bright, clever man—cleverer than I was when we was kids—but Nate, you got the wrong attitude."

Papa sighed. "Well, what about the poor devil that owes you money?"

"I'm trying to tell you."

Papa glanced at David, and David made believe he was fixing a knot in his shoelace.

"This feller made me an offer. He's got these two Fords that he worked on and turned 'em into one machine."

"One?" Papa looked puzzled.

"Yes. Hitched 'em together."

David had to speak up. "I read about somebody did that. They used it like a coach."

"That's it, Davey! You hit it on the nose. Holds eight people, and you got room on the back for luggage." He paused triumphantly and looked at his brother. "Don't that give you any ideas?"

"I can't say that it does." Papa knocked out his pipe in the fireplace.

Exasperated, Uncle Tom said, "That's your trouble, Nathan. You don't catch on to ideas. That old Ford camel with two humps would—make—a—dandy. . . ." He paused again for effect. ". . . taxicab!"

Papa shrugged. "Not a doubt in the world about that."

"And you run a taxicab, with an old broken-down horse." He pulled down the corners of his vest. "That Ford would make you a jim-dandy taxicab."

"I guess it would," Papa said. "But it's not me this man owes money to."

"No, but he owes it to me. And he's offered me that darned auto in payment for his bill. First I didn't know what in tarnation I'd want with a thing like that. I said to Eloise, who wants a think like that? Then I thought of you."

Papa refilled his pipe, tamping down the tobacco carefully. "I don't believe, Tom, that you are getting ready to give me this automobile."

"Not give it to you, no. I can't go around giving away

valuable things like that."

"And since I don't have any money, what are we talking about it for?"

"Because we can go into partnership, that's why."

Papa frowned. The blue flame of the kitchen match flared up as he lit his pipe. The sharp smell of sulfur made David's nose itch. "A partnership requires money from both partners."

"You can raise some money. We'll form a little company. If you can raise three hundred dollars, I'll put up the auto. We can work out something so I get a share of your profits, to make up the difference." He pulled a little notepad from his pocket. "I got some figures here. . . ."

"Tom," Papa said, "I could fly to the moon quicker than I could raise three hundred dollars."

"I could help a little, Papa," David said. Why was his father always so stubborn? It sounded like a wonderful idea, to get an auto.

His father looked at him but didn't answer him.

"What you could do, Nathan," Uncle Tom said, "is put it to your regular passengers about buying small shares in the company."

Papa looked at Uncle Tom in amazement. "And why would they want to do that?"

"Because they're businessmen. You've got a good little business here, getting better all the time, with the summer folks coming to Conomo and all." He made some quick marks on the pad. "Say you got six of them to put up fifty dollars each. There's your three hundred."

"And what do they get for their investment?"

"A share of the profits. That's the way they do, Nathan.

All them businessmen, they do that way."

Papa laughed. "By the time I get through paying everybody their shares, I'd be better off with old Lady."

Uncle Tom slapped his pencil down in irritation. "Nathan. How many times have you had to turn down passengers? How many times is it you haven't been able to accommodate because the old coach was full, or the old plug couldn't move along fast enough to get out to Conomo or down to Gloucester. . . . Why, balls of fire, man! With an auto you could get all over Cape Ann. Even do a little light hauling."

"Tom," Papa said, "you should have been a lawyer."

"I'm just a businessman, Nathan, that's all. Just trying to shake a little sense into my big brother. Now I'll tell you what we'll do. . . ." His words were lost in the loud bong-bong-bong of the clock. He glanced at it. "Why in thunder don't you get rid of that old clock of Pa's?" He took out his gold watch. "It don't even keep the right time."

Papa went over to it and opened the little door with the United States seal painted on the glass. He took out the key and began to wind the clock. He turned the key around and it slipped out of his fingers, clattering to the floor.

"Damned key doesn't work," he said. He seemed suddenly upset. "Maybe I should get rid of it."

"I can get you a nice new Seth Thomas, wholesale."

David picked up the key and got the pliers out of the hall closet. "The threads are worn on the key, that's all," he said, but neither of the men was listening to him. He squeezed the key gently with the pliers and then tried it on the clock. It worked. Maybe the men up at the blacksmith shop could make him a key.

"Don't give me an answer now," Uncle Tom was saying to Papa. "Just think it over and let me know first of the week."

After he and Aunt Eloise had gone, David heard his father telling his mother about Uncle Tom's idea. He was laughing about it. "Tom's got an idea a minute," he said.

Mama put away the dishtowel and sat down. She looked thoughtful. "Well, he makes money, Nathan. His ideas seem to work."

"He makes money, and I don't. Is that it?"

"You know it isn't. If you were like Tom . . . well, I wouldn't be sitting here." She got up and put her hands on his thin shoulders. "Don't be touchy. You're always touchy when Tom's been here."

"He makes me feel like a failure."

"You're not a failure." She leaned around and kissed his cheek.

David went out to feed Lady and the chickens. Papa *was* a failure, and he always would be because he wouldn't listen to reason. David kept thinking about the auto, and the more he thought about it, the more excited he got. If only Mama could talk Papa into getting it. But he knew Papa would never ask those men for money. He'd see it as asking a favor, instead of the way Uncle Tom saw it, offering to let them in on a good thing. If you were going to do it, David felt you'd have to tell them just how things stood, and that if they wanted to gamble their money, all right, but it would be a gamble. That way, you wouldn't be fooling anybody.

David got his pole and went off to light the lamps. All the

way along the main street and across the Causeway, he kept thinking about the auto. If they had one, he'd get to study the engine. He could learn how to fix it and save Papa money. And he'd learn to drive. As far as he knew, Papa had never even been in an auto. If David learned first, he could teach Papa, and then sometimes he might get to drive it himself. Maybe he could just sit in it and figure out how things worked.

It wasn't until he came back into his own yard that it occurred to him that if Papa got the auto, Lady would go.

7

All through the week no one mentioned the auto, and David decided there was no use thinking about it. A letter came for Papa from Uncle Tom, but neither Papa nor Mama said what was in it. Papa seemed unhappy and morose, and Mama tried to get him to go to the doctor about his arm. He refused.

"That arm's been bothering me all these years, and no doctor could fix it yet. Why throw money away now?"

"It seems worse," Mama said. "You favor it more, and at night when you roll over on that side, you groan, Nathan."

"You can't hold it against a man what he does in his sleep."

"Don't be silly. I'm not holding anything against you. I'm concerned about you, that's all." Mama's voice sounded annoyed. She was tired. She'd been to choir rehearsal, and every afternoon that week she'd worked with the chorus that was going to sing at the Fourth of July celebration. And there were the pupils nearly every day, and keeping the house, and feeding David and Papa. David was glad he wasn't a woman. They worked too hard.

"No need to be concerned about me," Papa said, and his voice too was unusually sharp. "I may not be a ball of fire like Tom, but we survive." He put his hat on the back of his head and went out.

Mama left the dishes in the sink and sat down at the kitchen table. "Sometimes," she said, "I just don't know."

David wasn't sure whether she was talking to him or to herself, so he waited but he didn't say anything. Then she looked up at him.

"I hope you and Andrew will remember, when you grow up and get married, that most women don't judge their husbands by how much money they bring into the house. A woman marries a man, not a bank account. Why can't your father understand that? He torments himself because we're poor. What do I care if we're poor? We have enough to eat, we've got our house, we've got you and Andrew. Why can't he see that?"

David felt that he should say something. Mama had never talked to him like this before. He tried to think what Andrew would say. "I guess it's because he's proud," he said. "Uncle Tom has everything. . . ."

She interrupted him impatiently. "Uncle Tom has nothing. He's got a prosperous business that's going to kill him one of these days. High blood pressure, heart attacks. . . . He's got a big house that he never has time to enjoy. He's got no children." She slapped her hand on the table. "Tom has *nothing*. They're the loneliest people I've ever known. I'm *sick* of hearing about Tom." She got up and poured herself a cup of coffee. "And your grandfather. The war hero. The great man, who spent what little time he was at home making his sons feel like failures." She took a deep, shaky breath and looked at David. "I suppose I shouldn't talk to you like this, Davey, but you're growing up now. I want you to learn what things are important."

"Sure, Mama." David felt uncomfortable. He had rarely seen his mother so upset, and the things she said amazed him. He'd always thought Uncle Tom led a wonderful life, and that his grandfather O'Brien was practically a god. He felt confused.

She leaned across the table unexpectedly and kissed him. "You're a good boy, David. But don't be *too* good. Don't make yourself a living sacrifice for anybody. There's too much martyrdom in this family."

David didn't know what she meant, but he nodded. He tried to think of a reason to go outdoors that wouldn't hurt her feelings. She anticipated him.

"You'd better feed the chickens. And see if the setting hen is all right. I'm too tired to move, and I think your father's gone. . . ." She hesitated, and for a moment he thought she was going to say "to Gloucester, to the saloon," but she didn't. ". . . gone downtown, I suppose," was all she said.

He wanted to go, to escape from hearing any more of this, and yet he lingered. "I didn't know you didn't like Grandfather O'Brien."

She pushed back the hair that curled against her cheek. "I didn't say I didn't like him. He was a charming, intelligent man, and obviously brave. But he never thought of any-

one else. Do you remember your grandmother?"

He tried to think. "Not very well."

"I'm sure you don't. She had turned into a shadow. Once she'd been very pretty, and she told me she loved to dance when she was young. . . ."

"Papa always says she was a saint."

She shrugged. "If being a saint means learning to erase yourself. She worked so hard at it that she became an invalid. Your father spent too much of his young manhood taking care of her while your grandfather strutted around the country wearing his medals and Tom went off to college." She broke off and shook her head. "I shouldn't talk to you this way. I'm ruining your idol. But I get so sick of idols. People destroy themselves serving idols that aren't real. Well, go feed the hens. And don't let the new hen go hungry; she hasn't found her place yet."

That night after he had gone to bed, David heard Papa come home. They talked a long time downstairs. Sleepily he wondered what they were talking about. An awful lot seemed to go on in families. He'd had no idea of all that about his grandparents and he'd never thought of Uncle Tom and Aunt Eloise as lonely. They seemed lucky, to him. He'd have to talk to Andrew about it some day.

Saturday at the yard they began framing up the new boat. Everybody came over to help when the foreman shouted: "Frame up!" except the man who was lettering the nameboard of the *Mildred W.*, doing it in gilt, and etching it with scroll work till it looked to David fine enough to be in a museum.

David stood between Pete Alzar and Horace Wesley, ready to help lift the ribs of the new vessel into place, getting the frame up onto the keel. It was a steaming, hot day, and David felt the sweat run down his back.

When the frames were fastened in place, they would look like the bones of a big fish. David felt fond of it; this one he would be working on all summer, long after the *Mildred W.* had slid down the ways and gone to sea. This one seemed like his own boat.

"There's your pa, Davey," Horace said.

David looked up and saw his father driving Lady along the Causeway, with a man and woman and two children in the coach. Summer people, David thought. He waved, and his father held up the whip handle. David wondered if he would say, "That's my son, working in the shipyard." Probably not. Papa wasn't much for saying things like that. The two children were leaning out, watching the men in the yards. Probably city kids, from Boston. If you took a taxi in Boston nowadays, it would most likely be an auto. Lady was limping a little bit. He'd go up to see Grandpa tomorrow and ask him what to do for her. He watched Papa's ramrod-stiff back as he drove the coach down the road.

8

That night for supper they had fresh clams, that Papa had bought from Mr. Woodman. Mama rolled them in cornmeal and fried them in deep fat till they were golden and crispy. David loved them, and he ate till he could hardly get up from the table. But somehow he managed to eat a big dish of Indian pudding too, with thick fresh cream on it.

"We're lucky you're such a good cook," he said to his mother.

"Only reason I married her," Papa said. "I wanted to give my son a mother who could cook."

David grinned. He liked it when Papa made jokes because that meant he was feeling good. He'd had a good week because a lot of the cottages at the Point had opened up. "We were talking about the summer people at choir rehearsal," Mama said. "Everybody says they're coming in droves."

"Good for business," Papa said.

Mama gave him a sidelong glance. "What a pity we can't afford an auto."

Papa shook his head and pushed back his chair. "Some men were born to cash in on the long chance," he said. "I'm not one of them."

"Nonsense," Mama said. "It's not what you're born to, it's what you make happen."

David decided to venture a comment. "With a machine, Papa, you could take summer people all over Cape Ann, even to Rockport."

"No doubt, boy. But a man needs capital." He got his pipe and went out to sit on the back doorstep.

It was a beautiful evening, with the sunset turning the sky pink and lavender and pale gold. David stepped over Papa's legs and went out to the barn. He had half an hour or so before lamplighting time. He led Lady out of her stall and went over her leg very carefully. The knee joint seemed to be swollen.

"You've done a lot of work in your time, old girl," he said. "I wish you could just take it easy now." But he couldn't see Papa paying for feed for a horse that wasn't working. Papa believed everybody had to pay his own way, one way or another. Mama said sometimes that for an Irishman whose parents had been Catholic, Papa was the worst Puritan she'd ever known. "Cotton Mather would hug you to his bosom," she'd say, and Papa would laugh and say, "I hope not."

David got a bucket of oats for Lady and let her stay outside for a while. He fed the chickens and made sure the new Rhode Island Red got her share. The big, bossy rooster sat on the post at the end of the chicken run, watching disdainfully while his hens ate.

Papa had been hoeing in the garden, between the rows of peas. They usually had peas for the Fourth of July, but it had been a late spring and they weren't quite ready. A week from next Saturday was the Fourth, and David would have two free days. He wished he had some firecrackers. Last year he'd been hired as a "firecracker boy" by the Wenham paper; he'd gone around getting subscriptions for them, and they'd paid him off in firecrackers. But this year there hadn't been time, and he couldn't spare any of his money for firecrackers. He pulled up a radish, brushed off the dirt, and ate it, gasping a little at its hotness. Summer was a good time because if money was short, you could just about live off the garden and the fishing. Pretty soon Mama would start canning stuff for winter, and the house would smell wonderful.

David lay on his back in the grass, watching the sunset and thinking about Andrew. Maybe when they were a little older, they could set up their own shipyard. David would supervise it, and Andrew would be in charge of the fishing fleet. Maybe they could make a lot of money and be comfortable. Sometimes the minister talked about money not being worth a hill of beans. David had thought about it, and he decided that was true if you were talking about money just for its own sake. But money could buy you the freedom to do what you wanted to do. It could buy you independence, so you didn't have to say aye yes or no to anybody. And you could do for your mother, so she didn't have to work so hard, and you could buy Grandpa those extra five acres he hankered after. And you could buy your father the auto, and if he didn't feel like going out to the station to pick up the people, he could hire somebody to do it for him. And you could put Lady out to pasture, where she could dream and eat and think about the good old days when she was a performer. He looked at the horse, wondering if animals remembered things like that.

He heard his father's deep voice, and an answering man's voice. He lifted his head to see who it was. Mr. Milliken, looking different in a white shirt with the sleeves rolled up over his big forearms, and a pair of old white-duck pants that made him look comfortable.

" 'Evening, Harvey," Papa said. "Take a seat."

Mr. Milliken lowered himself carefully onto the stone step beside Papa. " 'Evening, Nathan. Nice evening."

"Fine. Smoke?" Papa held out his old leather tobacco pouch.

"No, thanks, Nathan. The doctor made me quit. Says I huff and puff too much. Told him the reason I huff and puff is I'm too damned fat."

Papa laughed. "You look fine to me, Harvey. You're a big man—you don't want to go around all skin and bones, like me."

"I eat too much. I eat like a damned pig, Nathan."

"Well, you can't drive a big engine on no fuel."

Mr. Milliken was silent for a minute. "Funny you should put it that way, because that's what I came by to talk about."

"What's that?"

David felt a little guilty, lying there unseen in the grass, listening, but he was curious.

"Engines," Mr. Milliken said. "Machines."

"Oh?" Papa sounded puzzled.

Mr. Milliken sneezed, and there was a long interval while he got his handkerchief from his back pocket and blew his nose. "Hay fever. Gets me every year." He blew his nose again. "Well, somebody or other mentioned that you had a chance to go partners with your brother on some kind of a crazy automobile, two of 'em, they said, stuck together like a pair of love-bugs."

David could hear the change in his father's voice.

"Where'd you hear that, Harve?"

"Oh, lord, I forget. You know how people talk. Especially about other folks's business. Me included, I'm right in there with the rest of them. Anyway, it sounded like a good idea to me."

There was a long wait before Papa answered.

Finally he said, "The feller that told you that didn't finish the story."

"No, he didn't. I came by to hear how it ended."

David could smell the smoke from Papa's pipe.

"Just about like you'd expect. A man can't go partners with anybody if he don't have any money."

"The way I heard it, there was a way around that. Something about getting your regular passengers to invest—form a little corporation, you might say."

"Your source of information seems to be pretty good," Papa said drily.

David lay very still. He knew that Papa would be really angry now, if he caught him there listening. But it was too late to get up and leave; they'd see him. He tried to think who could have told Mr. Milliken about the auto. He was pretty sure Papa wouldn't have talked about it around town. Papa was close-mouthed about his personal affairs.

"I got it out of him," Mr. Milliken said. "I told you, I'm a born gossip." He sneezed again, three times, and blew his nose loudly. "I don't blame you for turning it down, Nathan. It wasn't a good idea."

Papa's voice sounded more friendly. "Agree with me, do you?"

"Sure. Too many cooks spoil the chowder. What you need is just one source of capital."

Again there was a pause before Papa answered. "I don't get you."

"Well, I'll get down to cases, Nathan. I want to make a deal with you. I'll buy the auto from Tom, free and clear. Then you and I'll take title on it jointly, fifty-fifty, even-Steven. You can figure out how much you need to take out of the profits to live on, and we'll work out a percentage for everything over and above that."

"You mean you want me to work for you?"

"You haven't been listening, Nathan. I want you and me to be partners."

"Why would you want to do a fool thing like that? A little two-bit business. . . ." Papa's voice grew angry. "If Tom's been trying to sell you on some kind of charity deal. . . ."

"Hold on, hold on. I haven't seen Tom in three, four years, haven't talked to him. I don't even know for sure he'd sell to me. . . ."

"Tom would sell anything to anybody."

"All right, then. What do you say to my proposition?"

"I know you mean well, Harvey, but you know I couldn't do a thing like that."

"Why not, for God's sake?"

"Because I'd be beholden to you."

Mr. Milliken sounded exasperated. "Nathan, you are shortsighted, pigheaded. . . ." He broke off. "Listen, Nathan—now you listen to me good. The age of the automobile is here. Everybody knows it. If Essex shuts its eyes to it, we may end up some little out-of-the-way backwater village. We got to get people in here, show folks we're part of the twentieth century."

Papa gave a dry little laugh. "You're a go-getter, Harvey, always was. Just like Tom."

"I look at the facts. I'm a businessman. I own property. Now, listen to me, Nathan, you think over what I've said. One way we can get summer people down here is with good service, and that don't mean carting them out to the Point in your old horse and buggy, no offense intended."

"None taken."

"All right. We need a public conveyance, a machine that'll get you there before you die of old age. I tell you the truth, I see this auto of Tom's as just a beginning. We may end up with a fleet of 'em, Nathan."

"I don't see that many people coming to Essex."

"We'll cover the whole Cape, man. Now you take the launching of the *Mildred W*. There's a bunch of important people, friends of the owner, coming down from Boston for the launching. How are they going to get from the depot to the shipyard? In your coach, with a horse that's going lame?"

"If they're so damned progressive up in Boston," Papa said, "let 'em drive down in their own machines."

"Oh hellfire, man, it would take all day. Be reasonable." He heaved himself to his feet, and David could see his shadow on the grass. "You think it over. And don't close up your mind like some damned tinderbox. Think ahead. It's for the good of the town, not just your own neck."

"I gave you my answer."

"I won't take it. You're mad as a wet hen because somebody spilled the beans to me and I'm not saying who it was. Being a private man is something I admire, Nathan, but by God, you do carry it awful far. I'll be back in a few days."

"You'll be wasting your time, Harvey."

"Good night," Mr. Milliken said cheerfully. "My boy's going lobstering tomorrow. If he has any luck, you want to buy a couple?"

"Yes. I'll buy a couple."

"Good night, Nathan."

"Good night."

David went on lying in the grass because he knew Papa was still sitting on the doorstep. But in a minute he'd have to get up and go light the lamps. He heard his mother come out.

"Was that Harvey Milliken?"

"Yep."

"I should have brought him out a cup of coffee. Did he want anything special?"

"Just passing the time of day."

"I see." The door creaked as she went back in.

Stiff from lying still so long, David rolled onto his side, and started to get up. In a second his father loomed over him, scowling angrily. David tried to look as if he'd just waked up from a nap.

"You been there the whole time?"

"I. . . ." He wanted to say he'd been asleep, but he'd never been able to look Papa in the eye and lie. "Yes. I didn't want to bother you. . . ."

Papa grabbed him by the shirt front and yanked him to his feet, his eyes blazing. "It was you told Harvey about Tom's auto. You put him up to it."

"No, Papa, I didn't." David tried to pull loose. The anger in his father's face alarmed him. "I never talked to anybody about it."

"You're lying."

"I don't lie to you, and you know it."

Papa hesitated, loosening his hold on David's shirt. "There's no other way he could have known, unless you've blabbed it all over town. . . ."

"Papa, I haven't told a soul. Not one." When his father didn't answer, he said, "I've got to go light the lamps."

"When you come back, we'll have a talk about this." Papa took hold of his injured arm as he often did when he was upset, as if it hurt him more then. "We'll get at the bottom of this. I can't stand a liar."

"Let the boy alone." It was Mama, standing on the step, looking tall and stern. "Let him alone, Nathan."

Papa wheeled around, surprised and annoyed at Mama's interference. "He's been telling my business around town. . . ."

"He hasn't told anything." She looked Papa hard in the eye. "I told Harvey's wife about the auto. We cooked up the whole scheme."

Papa's mouth opened in astonishment. "You? You never gossip. . . ."

"I wasn't gossiping. I was taking things in hand."

"You think I can't manage my own affairs?"

"I think sometimes you need a little push."

David hardly dared breathe as his parents stood there, now having forgotten about him, staring each other down.

"You ought to know by now," Papa said, in a cold, hurt voice, "I'm not a man to be pushed."

"Led, then." She lifted her hands in a quick, impulsive gesture and came to him. "Oh, Nathan, listen to the people who love you. Don't build your pride up around you like a stone wall. Let the dead past bury its dead; we're alive, the time belongs to us now."

David slipped away, into the barn, got his lamplighter's pole and went out the narrow back door of the barn. He was late. It was almost dark.

9

David got up early Sunday morning, before his parents were up. He was still smarting over the things Papa had said to him, accusing him of lying and all that. Papa was gone when he came back from lighting the lamps, and he still hadn't come home when David finally fell asleep. David's mother had looked as if she wanted to talk to him, but he'd said, "I'm going to bed, Mama. I'm tired," and she had let him go.

David went down the stairs, trying to skip the steps that creaked. In the kitchen there was a faint smell of stale beer that made him feel like gagging. Papa's hat was on the kitchen table. It was the old straw hat that Papa wore in the summer, the ribbon weather-stained and faded, the sweat-band pulled loose in the back. David looked down at it, and for reasons he didn't understand at all, he felt like crying. He picked it up, hung it on the hook where it belonged, and let himself out the back door.

He got the old bicycle he'd inherited from Andrew, and set off for Grandpa's house, up on the Hamilton side of Chebacco Lake. He pedaled fast, anxious to get away from home for a while, and wanting to see Grandpa, who was sometimes the only person you could talk to.

There was a low, ground-hugging fog that made him shiver at first, but the exercise soon warmed him up. Over his head, hidden by the fog, seagulls circled and squawked. When he turned into Pond Street, he hit a hole in the road and was almost thrown off the bike, but he got it straightened out again. It was foolish to ride fast when you couldn't see the ground, but he felt like being foolish.

By the time he got to the lake, the sun had begun to tatter the fog into thin strands. The woods were dense along both sides of the road, so not much sun could get through even if it was a clear day. He slowed down and wheeled to the edge of the lake to rest for a few minutes. He sat on the shore and skipped flat rocks on the smooth surface of the water. Last winter Grandpa had built an iceboat and had taken David with him to try it out. When you got a good windy day, that thing went so fast it took your breath away. They'd had a fine time.

Across the inlet near him the big icehouses loomed up. When he was a little boy, he'd wanted to be an iceman; the iceman always seemed to be twice as big and strong as other men, balancing those huge chunks of ice on the leather apron on his shoulders, swinging them off the ice cart and into the icebox with those big tongs. Chebacco Lake ice was famous all around, and way back when Papa was a boy, the railroad people had run the Essex branch line around by Chebacco Lake to get the ice-shipping business. Grandpa said Wenham Lake ice was even better, and it had been shipped to the royal palace in England. It seemed odd to David that the English couldn't come up with ice of their own.

David pulled a needle off the pitch pine near him and chewed on it, enjoying the pungent taste. A cloud of dough-birds wheeled across the lake like smoke, and disappeared. He was beginning to feel better. Only the mosquitoes that sang around his head prompted him to get up and get moving.

He rode more slowly now, looking for wild animals and birds. When he'd come through here at night, with Grandpa or Papa, he had almost always spotted a raccoon or two. Sometimes they came right out on the road to see who was passing by. Once Papa got a good snapshot of a raccoon.

David braked suddenly and peered up into a little stream that fed into the lake. A big bird perched precariously on a dead tree limb that spanned the stream. A bittern. He waited, watching, until the bird spread its wide wings and took off. People came in through these woods from time to time and shot a lot of birds. It made David sick. Some of the ladies in church had hats made out of real birds. It made Mama so mad that once at Ladies' Aid she had said that wearing a hat made from a bird seemed to her about the same as dangling an enemy's scalp from your belt. Mama had some beautiful sketches she'd made of birds in strange parts of the world, when she had traveled with her mother and father. David liked to look at them.

He came around the head of the lake and crossed the

Hamilton town line. Grandpa's place was just down the road. He'd bought it about ten years ago, when Grandma had started getting sick. Now that she was gone, he farmed it himself, living alone, experimenting with new kinds of crops. Grandpa had been a newspaperman most of his life, starting with dispatches about the War Between the States, for the *Boston Evening Journal,* when he was twenty-six years old. He'd traveled all over the world, Grandma with him, and Mama too until she was old enough to be left in a Boston boarding school.

David rode his bike over the bumpy little wooden bridge that spanned the brook in front of Grandpa's place and wheeled up to the front piazza. On the other side of the street the neighbor kids were tending the roadside stand where Grandpa sold his surplus vegetables, but Grandpa himself was not in sight. The two tomcats, Pistol and Bardolph, flanked the stone steps like animals carved of stone.

David heard a familiar sound, a creaky, cranking kind of sound, and he smiled. Grandpa was doing what he'd been doing on Sunday mornings for as long as David could remember: he was making ice cream. Even after Grandma died, he kept on doing it, feeding it to the neighbor children if his own family didn't come over, eating a prodigious amount of it himself.

David went around the long, low, white house, with its fresh-painted green shutters. Sure enough, there was Grandpa, his dark-rimmed glasses slipping down his long nose, cranking away on the old freezer. The noise of it kept him from hearing David's approach, and David stopped for a moment to enjoy the sight. Grandpa was very tall and

broadshouldered, with thick black hair that had no trace of gray. He looked, even to David, like a young man, although he said he was seventy-two. David whistled.

His grandfather looked up and a slow smile spread over his face. He stopped cranking and shoved his glasses up with the inside of his thumb, the way he always did. "David. Glad to see you. I thought I might have to eat this whole freezerful by myself."

David came over and squatted down beside him. "What kind is it?"

"Fresh strawberry. Berries right out of the garden. You picked a good day to come." He brushed away a tiny calico kitten and said, "Scat, Polly Peachum." The kitten leaped sideways and hid under Grandpa's jacket, which hung on one of the kitchen chairs he kept outside. The kitten's face peeked out at them, striped white on one side, orange on the other, with a black streak down the nose. The pupils of her green eyes were thin black marks in the sunlight. Grandpa laughed. " 'Tiger, tiger, burning bright. . . .' "

"She's a new one," David said.

"You haven't been up lately. She's six weeks old."

"I have, Grandpa. I was here the week she was born, with Mama."

Grandpa peered over the tops of his glasses, which had slid down his nose again. "So you were. Time does somersaults when you get old." He took out the dasher, heavy with the pink ice cream, and handed it to David.

Grandpa's ice cream was always so good, you couldn't decide which kind was best; it always seemed as if the one you were eating then had to be the best. "This is my favorite," David said. He ate quickly, before it could melt, and then ran his finger along the dasher to catch the drops.

"Those strawberries are the best I've had yet. You want to see 'em?" He got up, a little stiffly, and reached for the thick black hawthorn walking stick that he'd bought long ago in Ireland. He didn't need a cane; he just liked the feeling of one, he said.

He set the big can of ice cream to ripen, and then he took David out back of the barn where his vegetable garden was. Two other kittens, both black, scampered after them, and the big mother cat came out of the barn to keep an eye on them. Polish chickens and three young pheasants skittered out of their way. Grandpa raised exotic fowl. Once before Grandma died, he'd had a peacock, but it had made so much noise screaming, Grandma couldn't sleep, so he gave it to the Franklin Park Zoo in Boston.

David stopped to pick a few big ripe strawberries. They were sweet and warm with sunlight. They walked down the neat, weeded rows between the different kinds of beans, past the tomato and squash vines, the cucumbers.

"George Allen, up the road, tries to tell me cucumbers aren't fit to eat." Grandpa chuckled. "I peeled one and ate it in front of him, and he turned white as a sheet—thought I'd killed myself." He flipped a squash bug off a vine and stepped on it. "Your grandmother liked them with a little lemon juice and salt. I'll still say, though, that the samphire I get in the marsh is better in a salad." He pointed to a row of corn. "Something new. Golden bantam." He pushed the tassels aside. "Gold as a doubloon. A whole lot better than the white stuff. You know how to eat corn, though, don't you, David?"

David grinned. This was an old exchange between them. "Get a pot of salted water to a rolling boil. Pick the corn and run like hell for the kitchen, husking as you go. Pop the corn in the water and boil five minutes."

"And if you drop the corn on the way. . . ."

"Leave it there."

"And if you stub your toe and fall down. . . ."

"Don't come in for supper."

They both laughed. One of the things David liked about visiting Grandpa was that so many things didn't change. There were stories to be told, jokes to retell, things to see, that never changed. It made David feel safe. Even when he and Grandma were traveling all the time, whenever they came back, with new stories to tell, about Persia or Africa or New Zealand, places David and Andrew would have to look up in the atlas, still there were the old familiar things too. Once he'd mentioned it to Mama, and she said, "Father believes in continuity." At the time he hadn't known what she meant.

"I've got a nice leg of lamb that I bought from Mr. Daley yesterday," Grandpa said. "Got it cooking right now. Supposing we have that for our dinner, and some of my little new potatoes, and some fresh peas."

"That sounds good."

"And strawberry ice cream."

David helped Grandpa strip the peas into a pail. "Our peas aren't ready yet."

"Well, you're always a little colder over there."

"I didn't say hello to Pegasus," David said.

"You can see him after dinner. He's just about out of that good salt hay you and I got over to Parker River last

August. We'll have to go again this year if you have the time."

"We could go on a Sunday." David listened to the ping of the green peas, as his thumbnail released them from the shell into the enamel kettle. He thought back to the day last summer—they'd had garden peas then too, only it was the last of the season—when he and Grandpa had gone in the little buggy that Pegasus pulled so stylishly, up to the marsh by Parker River to get salt hay. A cool, beautiful day, with even the pesky greenhead flies not bothering them because of the cool breeze. They'd worked all morning, cutting the hay, and later they'd gone back and pitchforked it into "staddles," stacks that they carried above high water. They left it there till early winter, when Pegasus and Lady could pull the wagon out onto the frozen marsh and get it home. Some of it had gone to Essex for Lady. Grandpa had said that was the way his grandfather, "your great-great-grandfather," had done his haying.

On the day they cut it, they'd had lunch beside a tidal pool—big ham sandwiches and a bottle of Grandpa's homemade Concord grape wine—and then they'd lain on their stomachs looking into the pool at the minnows, the steel-blue mummichog, the black-banded killifish with yellow bellies, the sheepshead minnow, blue with yellow belly and fins, the ghost shrimp no more than an inch long, the tiny blue crabs. And overhead the herring gulls wheeled and screamed and then settled down, all staring in the same direction, as if they were watching a show. Grandpa had told him why a gull shakes his head the way he does—to get the salt drops off his beak. All the creatures have one way or another to handle the excess of salt that builds up. Golden plovers had flown over the marsh, and he and Grandpa had turned on their elbows to watch a harrier hunting the white-footed mice. On the edges of the marsh the cattails grew high, and off to the west there was an old cedar swamp, where the short-billed dowitcher hunted. They'd almost fallen asleep there, he and Grandpa, lying in the coarse grass, listening to the singing of the wind through the grasses, the small thunder of crabs alarmed by their presence, moving away, and overhead a clapper rail cackling loudly. It was the kind of day David stored up in his memory, hoping he'd remember every bit of it when he was a hundred years old. And just when David was almost asleep, Grandpa had said, "Davey, try to keep things clear in your head."

"What do you mean?"

"There are so many fine-sounding, romantic words—like honor, and pride, and patriotism, and duty. They're all valid, all right, but they have to be examined very, very closely, because sometimes they're booby-trapped. People get you to do things by waving those words in front of your nose, like the carrot and the donkey." He had lifted up on one elbow, staring up at the white clouds. "I went to a military funeral yesterday. A general, a man whose biggest battle I happened to be on hand to see, in the War Between the States."

"Did they have a color guard?" David asked sleepily.

"Oh, yes. And there's going to be a statue. Iron man on an iron horse, thrusting his iron sword straight up into God's face." He picked a piece of the coarse grass and chewed on it. "But I kept remembering a young lad who shared his canteen with me before the battle. A boy from Portland. Nice boy. About Andrew's age. Ten minutes later I saw a mini-ball cut that boy in half."

David shivered, thinking of Andrew.

"I still see that boy in my dreams." Grandpa had sat up straight, frowning, as if he saw him. "I suppose Attila the Hun was a brave man. None braver than Napoleon. But you have to ask what it's *for*." He'd gotten up then, looking very tall as David looked up at him. "Thank God when I die, there will be no color guard."

Now, watching Grandpa dump the green peas into the kettle of boiling water, David said, "Do you remember last year at Parker River how we saw the dance of the fiddler crabs?"

Grandpa smiled and nodded. "I remember 'em." He stepped back as the three kittens raced across the floor, making a sound like faraway thunder. "When I was out West, we'd put our ears to the ground sometimes and hear the buffalo running, many miles away. It sounded the way the kittens sound." He scooped up one of the black ones and put him on his shoulder. David wished he could make a list of all the places Grandpa had been, and go there himself.

They ate dinner at the big trestle table in the long, dark-paneled dining room. Grandpa always used the good silver and the Spode china when company came, just as Grandma would have done. He liked to cook, and if no one else was coming for Sunday dinner, he'd often invite the children from across the street.

David ate the crisp-skinned roast lamb, the potatoes and

peas from the garden, the salad, and ice-cold milk from the big pewter pitcher.

"Mrs. Jewett bakes my bread for me," Grandpa said, pushing the plate toward David. "Very good bread. And Billy Jewett churns the butter."

When he brought the heaping plates of strawberry ice cream, he went to the kitchen once more and came in with a bottle of elderberry wine and two crystal wine glasses. He always let David pull the cork on a new bottle of wine. He tasted a little in his glass, the way Grandpa had taught him.

"Is it satisfactory?" Grandpa asked solemnly.

"An excellent bouquet," David said. That was what Grandpa always said.

"Your grandmother always said my elderberry was my finest work." He lifted his glass. "To your grandmother."

As David lifted his glass, he saw Grandpa's eyes shine with tears. He looked away, feeling his own eyes sting. Grandma had been dead almost three years, but he still missed her very much. She had been very pretty even in old age, and her soft South Carolina accent had enchanted him. She was a violinist, and David used to love to lie on the big Persian rug, listening to Mama and Grandma play duets, while Grandpa, in his big, carved wooden chair from Mexico, smoked his cigar and nodded his head in time to the music. It was terrible that people had to grow old and die. Some day, Grandpa. . . . David got up abruptly from the table, unable to finish the thought.

When they had cleared the table and done the dishes, Grandpa washing, in one of Grandma's lace-edged aprons, and David wiping, they went into the parlor to look at the things. Looking at the things was one of the good reasons for visiting Grandpa. In the big parlor, across the hall from the smaller and more comfortable sitting room, Grandpa had had shelves built all around the walls, some of them open, some of them protected by glass fronts. One whole wall held books, sets of leather-bound classics, travel books, a whole shelf of books on philosophy, a set of nature books, Dickens, Thackeray, Ruskin, Swift, Emerson, Thoreau, all sorts of books that David loved to look at. Some he was allowed to borrow, some, first editions, he could look at but not take home.

On the other shelves were the things Grandpa and Grandma had collected in their world travels. Sometimes Grandpa walked around the room with David, telling him the little stories that went with different things; sometimes he just stood by the door or sat on the deacon's bench in the middle of the room. It was like going to a museum, only better because Mama said that someday all these things would belong to Andrew and David. David liked to think about showing them to his own children and grandchildren: "This is the boomerang that Grandpa got from the aborigines that time in Australia, when he was writing a series for the *New York Sun*. This is the right foreleg of a wildebeest in the Serengeti. This is a little sketch Mr. Monet made for Grandma, when she and Grandpa were visiting her brother, who was an attaché at the embassy in Paris. This is the manuscript of a short story by Gail Hamilton, Grandpa's first cousin, who was a famous writer and lived right here in Hamilton. Her real name was Abigail Dodge, and she lived in Washington, D.C., a lot, as friend and confidante of James G. Blaine." Whenever Grandpa had said that about Gail Hamilton and James G. Blaine,

Andrew had winked at David, trying to make him laugh. Once Grandpa had caught him and said, "Scrub out your mind, Andrew. Cousin Abigail was pure as the driven snow." Then he had glanced at Grandma and added, "At least I think she was."

Today Grandpa stood near the fireplace, letting David wander around the room by himself. Grandpa leaned a little on his hawthorn stick, as if he felt tired, and he was looking up at the painting of Grandma that hung over the fireplace. It had been painted when she was a young Charleston belle, just before she met Grandpa, and, as he liked to remember, "told me to my face I was a miserable Yankee dog." The fine, wavy hair that David remembered as silver, had been black then, piled high on her head. Her dark eyes danced with humor, as they had all her life.

"Beautiful, wasn't she," Grandpa said.

"Yes. She and Mama are the most beautiful ladies I've ever seen."

Grandpa put his arm around David's shoulders and they went into the sitting room. "How's your father?"

Suddenly David was telling him the whole story, about Lady, and the automobile, and Papa's drinking. Grandpa listened gravely. "Well," he said finally, "I suppose Nathan will have to give in. If he doesn't get a machine, someone else will. That man in Dearborn is going to see to it that his smelly, noisy machines engulf the land."

"Don't you like autos, Grandpa?"

"I hate them."

David was surprised. Grandpa was usually very up-to-date. "Why?"

"Machines will be the death of us." He tipped his head

back against the cool leather of the chair. "Went up to Lawrence a while ago and saw those woolen mills. Women and little children, David, going to work when it's still dark, working till after nightfall in those wicked mills. It's like a scene from Dickens. Machines will be the death of us."

"Mama wants Papa to get the auto."

"She's thinking of the children."

David stared at him. "What children? Grandpa, Andrew is grown and gone, and I'm working in the yard. There aren't any children now."

"There are always children." Then Grandpa brought his gaze back to David's face. "You're right, Davey. I get time mixed up some days. Of course you're grown-up."

Just before David left, Grandpa went into the parlor again and brought back something in his hand. He held it out to David. "This is the tip of the bayonet that killed Crazy Horse. I'm giving it to you."

David couldn't believe it. That and the picture of Crazy Horse were among Grandpa's favorite relics, and he always told how he happened to be there when they brought in Crazy Horse and murdered him in cold blood. Crazy Horse had been trying to save his people and the white men killed him. The piece of steel, flattened, dull, only a little sharp now at the point, felt cold in his hand.

"There," Grandpa said, "was a truly great man. A brave man."

David knew that somewhere between the Ford taxi and the piece of steel that killed Crazy Horse there was a connection in Grandpa's mind. He would just have to puzzle over it and see if he could find it.

When he got on his bicycle to go home, Grandpa said, "Don't be too hard on your father, Davey. He's trying his damndest to stay an honest man. That's a whole lot harder than you might think." He patted David's shoulder. "Tell your mother to come see me soon."

David was almost to the lake before he remembered that he hadn't gone in to say hello to Pegasus.

10

They had Tod Milliken's lobsters for supper.

Papa cracked the big red claw with the nutcracker and said, "The good Lord must have favored New Englanders, putting them right next to the home of the lobster." Delicately he pried out the firm red meat and dipped it in melted butter.

"Lots of good tom-alley in this one," Mama said. "Eat the johnnycake while it's hot."

"I must have told you," Papa said, "about the time this feller from California tried to tell me they had lobsters." He looked at David, who grinned and waited for the familiar story. "Turned out what he was talking about was crawfish. Not the same thing, by a damned sight. But you couldn't convince him."

"Was that your partner, up by Leadville?" David asked, although he knew the answer.

"That was him." Papa broke off one of the tiny claws

and sucked out the sweet, watery meat, then broke the claw at its segments to get it all. "Stole all the gold we'd panned and all the provisions, and left me up there with a raging fever. Thought I'd die and save him a lot of trouble. I would have too, if that Arapaho hadn't come along and taken care of me. From that day to this I won't stand for hearing anything mean said about an Indian."

David took the steel fragment from his pocket and put it on the table. "Grandpa gave me the tip of that bayonet that killed Crazy Horse."

Mama looked up in alarm, but she didn't say anything.

Papa picked it up and hefted it in the palm of his hand. "If it was anybody but Orrin, I'd say it was a fake."

"If Father said that was it, then that was it," Mama said.

"That's what I said. I never knew Orrin to tell a lie."

"That's what he said about you," David said impulsively. "I mean he said you were an honest man."

His father looked up with such a radiant smile, David looked away. "How did he come to say a thing like that?"

More and more often lately David found himself deeply moved without knowing what moved him. "Well, we were talking about the Ford taxi."

Papa shot a look at Mama. "And he thinks I shouldn't get in on it?"

"Well, he didn't say that. He said if you don't do it, somebody else will. But he said you were trying your damndest to be an honest man, and he said that was an awful hard thing to do." David looked and saw tears in his father's eyes. You didn't very often see Papa with tears in his eyes.

Papa got up from the table. "I'm going to paint the lobster pots," he said to Mama. "There's a family summering out at Cross' Island that asked me about lobsters. They'd like a big mess of them every weekend. I asked around, and it seems like there's a lot of folks that want 'em. I don't think Woodman can supply them all." He shrugged. "Might as well give it a try."

David went out later and helped Papa with the lobster pots, helping nail down the spruce slats over the three-foot wooden frames where they had come loose. After the paint dried, they would put on the net heads that let the lobsters into the traps. When he'd finished nailing the broken pots, David repainted the buoys in the yellow and blue colors that would tell other fishermen these were Papa's traps.

"It's not the best time to go out," Papa said. "They're still molting, most of 'em, but I'll give it a try." He picked up a length of warp line and looked at it critically. "I'll need some more line."

"Next weekend's the Fourth," David said. "I could go out with you." He loved to go out in the big dory, rowing down the river and out to the open sea, with the salt spray soaking him through and the boat riding the trough of the sea.

"All right. I could use some help." Papa looked at him. "I'm sorry I called you a liar."

David ducked his head in embarrassment. "That's all right."

"It's my damned temper. I act first and think later. You're not a boy who lies." He too turned his face away, as if the conversation embarrassed him. "I got two good boys, and

I'm thankful to the Lord." Then changing the subject with relief, he said, "How did your grandfather seem?"

"Fine. Same as always."

"You scared your mother when you told about the bayonet tip."

David was surprised. "Why?"

"That steel is one of Orrin's prize possessions. I could see her thinking he wouldn't have given it away unless he thought he might die."

It astonished David that his father could see all that in his mother's face. "I don't think he thought anything like that. I think he was trying to tell me something, but I'm not sure what it was."

Papa chuckled. "That's Orrin. He's deep." He stood up and put the paintbrush in the can of turpentine. "Well, we'll let 'em dry."

When David got up the next morning, Papa had made his trip to the depot and had already gone out in the boat to set his traps. He wouldn't have to go very far out, this time of year.

"Saw your pa goin' out with his lobster pots," Horace said, when David got to the yard.

"Yeah." David didn't say that he was going to try selling lobsters to the summer people. No sense giving everybody the same idea.

It was a blazing hot day, and David thought it would never end. Toward noon he saw Papa row up the river and tie up the boat. It must have been hot as Hades out there on the water.

After dinner there was a sudden commotion. Men were

running down the street, shouting something, and Old Joe, the junkman, was standing up on the seat of his wagon yelling.

"Go see what it is, Davey," the foreman said.

The bell in the Congregational Church began to ring before David got to Old Joe. It was the fire alarm.

"Big fire!" Old Joe yelled at David.

"Where?"

"Big fire!"

"Where is it, Joe?"

"Icehouses. Chebacco."

David raced back to tell the men, who were already starting to leave the yard to help. "Chebacco," David shouted. "The icehouses."

Papa had always told Andrew and David to stay away from fires; he was afraid they'd get hurt, the way he had. But this time it was different. The icehouses weren't far from Grandpa's place. That was reason enough to go along.

"Lord, this is a bad time for a fire," Pete Alzar said. "Everything's awful dry." He trotted out into the road and waited for the South Essex engine, named Essex Number Two, already being pulled up the Causeway. Men came running out of their houses, some still carrying their rubber boots.

David stood watching for a moment.

"Get your horse and come on along, Davey," one of the joiners yelled as he ran by him. "We'll need all hands to keep it from spreading to Hamilton."

David raced down the street to his house. He passed the men hitching up the other fire engine, the Amazon, to the streetcar that had been ready to leave for Crooked Lane Hill in Hamilton.

Nobody was around at his house, and he remembered that Mama had gone to play the piano for a rehearsal. He threw a halter over Lady's head and said, "Come on, girl. We've got to look out for Grandpa." He was glad Papa wasn't there to stop him. He hoped he wouldn't be mad. Papa always used to say Andrew could find more excuses to go to a fire than the devil himself could find for *his* activities. Usually David had stayed at a safe distance. Fires scared him. They were exciting, all right, with the flames shooting up, and the black smoke billowing, and everybody squirting water at the flames and yelling. But they always ended up in black, evil-smelling destruction, and that depressed him. He'd seen whole families burned out of house and home, nowhere to go but the Poor Farm. A boy in his class at school had been burned out, and the family just drifted away, nobody knew where.

He rode Lady along the road behind the electric car that was pulling old Amazon. They went past the big, ugly town hall that Mr. T.O.H.P. Burnham had left the town the money for, back in the 1890s. It was a place David liked, because of the library. For a second, he wished he could go in and find a good book, maybe that book called *Typee* that Grandpa had told him about. But then he heard yells behind him, and he saw the Essex II catching up. There was always a lot of rivalry between South Essex and Essex, and the fire engines were part of it.

"Hurry up!" David yelled to the Amazon. But the streetcar was already going as fast as it could go. It was a pretty good bet that the men pulling the Essex II would tire out before they got to the lake, and the Amazon would win. For the moment, people weren't thinking so much about the fire as they were about who would win the race.

The Essex II pulled ahead for about a quarter of a mile, and then the Amazon made its steady way into the lead, the trolley bell clanging, and men pushing whenever it came to an upward incline. The Amazon was still ahead when they got to the junction, where the tracks veered off toward Ipswich. During the time it took to unhitch the Amazon from the electric car and get it going under manpower, the Essex II surged into the lead again.

Aside from the excitement of the race, David had his mind on Grandpa. The woods and fields were awfully dry this summer, and a fire could spread with terrible speed. If anything happened to Grandpa's house and all Grandpa's wonderful things . . . and to Pegasus and the cats. . . . But he reassured himself that Grandpa would at least get the animals out of there if there were any danger. David didn't even let himself think, If anything happened to Grandpa. . . . But when Pete Alzar yelled, "Davey, give us a hand here with your horse," he didn't hesitate to help them hitch Lady to the long line of horses and men that were pulling the engine.

Things went well until they were just about at the foot of the lake. Then the two lead horses, Lady and Matt Harrison's black hunter, stumbled in a rut that was hidden by an accumulation of dust and debris. David, with his hand on Lady's halter, tried to help her, but she whinnied with pain and held up her rheumatic leg. David's heart sank. He never should have got her into this. While Matt and the others straightened out the other horses, he quickly untied her. "She's hurt her leg," he said to Matt.

Matt glanced at Lady quickly. "That's a shame." But the men were yelling at them to get moving, and everyone was running back and forth trying to get the team started.

David led Lady to the side of the road and watched both engines go down the road. He was torn between worry about grandfather and concern about Lady. Finally he took her a little way into the woods and tied her to a birch tree where there was some grass. "Listen, I'll be back in just a little while. And don't worry. If the fire starts this way, I'll be here before you're in any danger." He put his face against her shoulder. "I'm sorry I did such a damfool thing. In *Black Beauty* the groom says, 'Ignorance is the worst thing, next to wickedness,' and that's how I acted—ignorant." He lingered a moment longer, reluctant to leave her behind, but it would be worse to make her walk while her leg hurt.

Finally he ran down the road, tripping in the deep tracks the engines had made in the dry gravel. Already he could smell smoke and feel the increased heat in the air. He heard men shouting and horses neighing, and as he came around a bend in the road he saw the fire. It was Mr. Mears's icehouse, and the smoke was pouring out, as Papa would say, "to beat the band." The firemen were unrolling the hoses from the huge spool-shaped wooden frame they were rolled on, and some men ran down to the lake to fill buckets. But the icehouse was a very big building, wooden, with boardwalks all around it where the blocks of ice were snaked along either into or out of storage. Beyond the Mears build-

ing was the Story icehouse, and as David watched, sparks from the fire caught on the roof.

"There goes the Story house!" The cry went up, all along the lakeshore, and the men worked faster than ever, coughing in the heavy black billows of smoke. David joined in, carrying buckets of water, but it seemed to him like putting out the fires of hell with a teacup.

The firemen got the hoses connected and began to direct the water at the flames. The stench, as parts of the burning buildings fell in a wet sizzling mess, was sickening.

Somebody yelled at David to help with a hose, so he dropped his bucket and got his shoulder under the heavy hose. He was intent on what he was doing, but far back in his mind was the driving idea that they had to get the fire out before it set fire to the fields that led to Grandpa's place.

Lady would be all right, the wind was the other way.

When the Story icehouse too was a blazing mass of flames, they heard a welcome sound: the piercing toot of the engine that pulled the steamcars. A yell of relief went up from the exhausted men, the men of the Amazon and the men of Essex II, who were now not divided by any rivalry.

"They're sending their firefighter," one man yelled.

And in a few minutes the firefighter unit of the Boston and Maine Railroad chugged into sight. Men ran to help them get the hoses down to the lake.

The air was thick with heat and smoke, and sections of the icehouses lurched and crashed. Melting ice sent dirty, sawdust-laden water out onto the ground. Somebody yelled, and David ran as one of the big covered runways that led from the boardwalk to the top of the icehouse buckled and crashed with a great roar. Flames shot out from it, lighting up several pine trees nearby. A shower of soot fell on David's head.

"Don't get too close to that thing, Davey," Pete Alzar said in his ear. "You watch yourself."

The Mears building was so far gone, the men pulled the heavy hoses over to the Story building, hoping to save it, but it was already doomed. When sections of its honeycombed front fell away, David could see the sea of fire inside. He found he was coughing, and it was hard to breathe. The streams of water from the hoses seemed to make no impression at all, except to make more smoke.

David ran around to the back of the Story building, to see whether the woods were on fire. There were hundreds of people swarming around the place, some working, some just watching. He saw Pegasus on the other side of the road, hitched to Grandpa's little buggy with the gold-leaf trim, but he didn't see Grandpa anywhere. He must have come over, as a lot of Hamilton people had, to see if the fire was going to spread their way.

David jumped, as a dead pine near him suddenly burst into a torch. Cinders scorched his face. He had always thought, in the back of his head, that Papa must have been careless or clumsy to get hurt in the Giddings fire—people went to fires all the time without getting hurt—but now he saw how quickly something could happen. Everything was wild and out of control. You couldn't watch out for things because you didn't know they were going to happen. He hoped Grandpa would stay back out of the way.

For a moment he was almost alone, looking up at the

back of the blazing icehouse. Most of the men were around in front or on the sides, trying with little success to fight the fire. David stood still to get his breath, although it was hard to breathe at all. Looking up, he thought he saw something move along the railing of the first level. A long-handled, two-pronged hook that the icemen used for pulling the ice blocks along had been left leaning against the rail, and as David watched, something alive moved along the rail and pushed over the icehook. He watched it fall to the ground. He looked up again, trying to make out what it was that had pushed it. A squirrel, maybe? But surely a squirrel would know better. . . . He had seen both animals and birds fleeing from the area. Suddenly as a breeze lifted the smoke, he saw that it was a cat. A big, gray cat, crouched on the rail, too frightened to move. That particular part of the platform was not yet burning. Without stopping to think, David ran up the runway.

He heard somebody yell at him, but if he was going to get the cat, he had to do it fast. The runway had partly burned and the fire had been put out there, but David felt it sway as he ran up the wooden ramp. "Hold still, cat," he said between his teeth. "I haven't got much time."

The cat, frozen with fear, clung to the joist where he was perched. He was a big tomcat with one ear half-chewed off. David had to pull hard to get him loose. The stench of the drowned fire was sickening. He could hear people yelling at him, and he thought he heard Grandpa's voice. Finally he got the big cat in his arms, clutched against his chest, and he turned to run back to the ground. At the same time that the yelling increased, he felt the ominous lurch under him and saw the lower part of the runway start to buckle. He jumped and landed with a jarring smash in a patch of burned-over weeds.

For a moment neither he nor the cat moved. Then the cat howled, raked his arm with his claws, and leaped free. When David got to his feet, Grandpa was there, and so were Matt and Horace and Pete, and a handful of people he didn't know. He heard the crash as the whole runway collapsed.

Grandpa helped him to his feet. "You all right, boy?"

David nodded. The jolting fall had winded him.

"You've got. . . ." Matt surveyed him in disgust. "I swear to God, you've got the mental brains of a dim-witted chicken that ain't going to live to grow up. What did you do a fool thing like that for? Scaring your grandpa into a shock. . . ."

"He didn't scare me into anything," Grandpa said. He took David by the arm. "We'd better get home."

"For a damned old alley cat that ain't worth the swill he eats," Matt said, shaking his head as if he couldn't get over it.

"Let the boy be," Pete said. "Boys like animals, that's all. Didn't want to see the cat get killed."

"Animals! That ain't no animal. It's just a mean old tom. Look how he scratched the kid's arm. That's a thank you for you."

Horace laughed. "Come on, Matt. I'll buy you a beer. This fire's just got to burn itself out."

David felt foolish. He knew what he'd done had been reckless. If he'd gotten himself killed, or badly hurt, they'd all have felt bad. He followed Grandpa out to the road and got in beside him in the buggy. Pegasus had his red pompon woven into the harness behind his ear, and the ivory-handled buggy whip that Teddy Roosevelt had given Grandpa was in the whip socket.

"I've got to get Lady." He told Grandpa what had happened.

"We'll drive you down there, and then you better come over to my place. I'll ring up Doc Crane to come have a look at her. And we better do something about that scratch."

"Oh, it's all right." David glanced sideways at his grandfather. "I know that was a dumb thing I did."

"It was a noble impulse," Grandpa said. "Foolish but noble."

"I'm sorry I scared you."

"Oh, I'm not so close to annihilation as that young Matt thinks." He pulled gently on the reins to guide Pegasus around the wagons and fire engines that filled the road. The little black horse stepped along through the thick black mud left by the fire hoses as daintily as if he had been on an elegant graveled drive.

They found Lady gazing off through the trees, a wisp of grass hanging from her mouth, unperturbed by the commotion on the road near her. Grandpa got out and looked at her leg. "Well, I'm no judge, but she might have sprained it."

"That's the one she favors, the rheumaticky one."

"You hitch her up to the back of the buggy, and we'll go slow."

Lady limped badly, but she seemed able to walk without

too much pain. They stopped often to let her rest on the mile between the icehouses and the farm.

Grandpa hitched her to the iron ring outside the barn door. He made David wash the blood off the scratch the cat had made. "Wash it good, now, even if it hurts. Soap is a good antiseptic." He took the receiver off the hook of the phone that hung on the kitchen wall. "Central? Central? Get me Doc Crane, will you please? . . . I don't recall his number. You look it up for me, Mabel, that's a good girl. . . . No, Pegasus is all right. It's my grandson's horse. Hurt her leg. . . . Fire's just about out, now that both icehouses are gone." He waited a minute. "Dr. Crane? This is Orrin Andrews. My grandson's here with his father's horse. She's got a bum leg. . . . Well, she's been having some trouble with it, and just now she was helping pull the Essex fire engine and she stumbled in a rut. Might be a sprain, I suppose. Could you take a look? . . . Fine. . . . Yes, the fire's out. Burned flat, both icehouses. . . . Bad loss, yes. . . . Fine. Thank you." Grandpa hung up the receiver. "That man talks to beat everything. Talk, talk, talk."

Very carefully he examined David's scratch. "That kitty really ripped you up."

"He was scared, I guess."

Grandpa set about making tea from the boiling water in the copper kettle on the stove.

"I don't know what we'll do if Lady can't pull the carriage," David said. "Papa'll sell her to the glue factory."

"I don't think it will come to that."

"He said he would. He'll do anything for a little money."

Grandpa glanced at David. "Your father's not a mean

man, David. He just tries to make do. He wants to send you to college. . . ."

"College!"

"Yes. He's talked to me about it. He wants you to get ahead in the world, have a good life, be a professional man."

David was amazed. "He never said that to me."

"Well, so far he hasn't seen his way clear to promise you anything. But he's working at it."

David thought Grandpa must be mistaken, but he didn't like to say so. "Maybe he just thought it up when he was drinking." He was sorry as soon as he'd said it.

Grandpa got out two china cups and then went to the stove and poured the tea. "You're old enough now to understand about your father's drinking, David. He's not a drunkard, not by a long sight. He's an unusual man, your father is, an intelligent, sensitive man who's had the cards stacked against him a good deal of the way. He's an honest man, and he holds onto his integrity and his principles even when anybody with eyes in his head can see he's dead wrong. . . ." He broke off and shook his head. "You've got to respect a man for doing what he thinks is right, even if he's stubborn as a mule. And Nathan is stubborn as a whole twenty-mule team. But I like the man. I respect him." He put the teacups on the table. "I don't hold with excessive drinking, but he does it now and then when things get too much for him. And he has a lot of pain, you know."

"I know it."

"Well, be tolerant, Davey. Try to understand him. He loves you and Andrew very much."

"Just the same, if I've ruined Lady, taking her to a fire

when he's told me never to go, he's really going to take out after me."

"Off hand, I'd say he had a right to."

David blinked. Grandpa didn't usually scold.

Grandpa bent his head to look out the window. "Here comes Dr. Crane."

"And that's another thing. Papa said he wouldn't pay a vet."

"I'll take care of that. No need to aggravate Nathan about that."

"I'll pay you back, Grandpa."

Grandpa got up, drinking the rest of his tea in a long swallow. "I'll take it out of your hide when we go haying."

When they got out in the yard, Dr. Crane was already examining Lady. "This mare is getting on in years," he said.

"She's an old circus horse," Grandpa said. "My son-in-law uses her to pull the taxi in Essex."

"She's not going to be pulling any more taxis," the vet said.

David's chest felt tight. He could just imagine what Papa was going to say. "Is it a sprain or what?"

"Well, yes, she sprained it when she stumbled, but she's worn out. Too old for work." He rubbed Lady's neck and she bent her head to look at him curiously. "Good old girl. Good pony." He lifted her leg and bent the knee. She whinnied and started away. "All right. I won't do that again." He looked at Grandpa. "I'll give you a bottle of liniment, and I'll bandage that knee to help ease the sprain. Don't let her move around for a week or so. Then if I was you, I'd put her out to pasture."

To hide his distress, David leaned against Lady's neck.

"Poor Lady. Poor girl," he murmured. She rolled her eyes around at him, and then, staggering a little, lifted her front feet and pawed the air with her good leg, bowing her head up and down.

"Say," Dr. Crane said, "that's all right! Can she do a lot of tricks like that?"

"She used to," David said.

"My kids would like to see that. Tell you what, Mr. Andrews, when the pony feels a little better, if you'll let my kids come see her do a few tricks, we'll call it square on the bill."

"You'll have to ask David," Grandpa said.

"Sure," David said. "That's fine." He wouldn't have to worry about the bill then. "Tell them to come on a Sunday, when I'll be here."

"Fair enough."

"Crane, do you happen to know a big gray tomcat around here, with fur torn off his shoulder and one ear half-gone?"

"Sure. That's the McDavitts' cat."

"He isn't rabid, is he?"

"Wasn't, as of yesterday forenoon, when I had to sew up his shoulder."

"My grandson saved him from getting killed, over to the icehouse fire."

Dr. Crane looked at David. "No favor to the town of Hamilton. That cat can be heard for twenty miles, and he's torn up so many males, I've lost count."

"I just wanted to make sure he wasn't rabid. He gave the boy a deep cut."

"That sounds like him." Dr. Crane looked at David's

arm. "You hold still, and we'll fix that." He got a bottle out of his buggy. "It'll sting like fury for a minute."

David gritted his teeth. It did sting like fury. He tried to thank Dr. Crane but the vet and Grandpa were talking about the fire. David went into the house and sat in one of the kitchen chairs, waiting for the fire in his wrist to quit.

Grandpa came in at last. "Told you he was a talker. Your arm still hurt?"

"A little."

"I'll carry you over to the Junction and you can take the electric car home." He put his foot on the seat of one of the chairs. "Your father's got to have some way to go get his passengers." He frowned, thinking. "Mose, over at the livery stable, owes me a little money. I'll ring him up and get him to let your father have one of his horses for a week. That'll give Nathan time to work something out." He shook his head. "This is going to be a shock to him."

When David finally sank onto the seat of the trolley, he was tired out. But the day wasn't over, by a long shot. He was going to have to tell Papa that Lady couldn't work any more.

11

He had to tell Papa right away. On the streetcar ride he had rehearsed his speech a hundred times. He could say, "Well, Papa, you said yourself Lady was worn out. . . ." But Papa would get mad. One of the things that was going to make him maddest was that David had gone to the fire when he wasn't supposed to; and that he had taken Lady made it worse; and that he had hitched Lady to the engine was the worst of all. It had all happened so fast, with everybody yelling and telling him what to do, he hadn't even stopped to think, but now when he thought about it, he couldn't imagine how he could have done such a thing. Papa had a right to get mad. But just the same, he didn't want him to. He might get a licking, big as he was, but that wouldn't be the worst of it. The worst of it was, Papa would be left without a way to run the taxi, when they needed that money to live. And it would be David's fault, not Papa's. David kicked the wooden seat in front of him in frustration.

If only he was old enough to earn some real money.

He got off the streetcar and ran all the way home, hoping Papa hadn't heard the worst from anybody else. Both Papa and Mama were in the yard when he ran in. He saw the worry in both their faces change, Mama's to relief, Papa's to anger. So they'd heard something.

Papa started talking right away. "I told you never to go fire fighting. I've told you boys all your lives. . . ."

"I'm sorry, Papa. . . ."

" 'Sorry' don't cut any ice. I mean what I say when I tell you something."

"We were so worried," Mama said. "We heard you went, and then you didn't come home."

"I went to Grandpa's."

"Where's Lady?" Papa said.

"What happened to your arm?" Mama said, taking his hand. "Where did you get that terrible scratch?"

"Oh, an old tomcat. . . ."

"Nathan, he could get hydrophobia!"

"No, Mama, Grandpa had the vet fix it. He knows the cat; it isn't wild."

"The vet!"

"David," Papa said. "Where's the horse?" His voice was ominously quiet.

"Papa, she's out of commission. It's my fault. I hitched her up to the fire engine, with the other horses, and she stumbled in a hole and sprained her knee. The vet says she's too old to work anyway; she ought to be put out to pasture. Just like you said, Papa, she's too old to work any more."

Papa stared at him. "Where is she?"

"She's over to Grandpa's. She's all right; she isn't in any pain." David talked as fast as he could. "Grandpa rang up Mose, because Mose owes him some money, and Mose will let you have a horse for a week, so you'll have time to figure out what you want to do." He stopped talking because he couldn't think of anything to say. He was frightened because Papa wasn't losing his temper. He didn't even look mad; he just looked white, as if he was sick.

Mama began to talk, in the fast, cheerful voice she used when things were going wrong. "Well, that will give you time then, Nathan. Something had to be done anyway. It's a good thing Mose owed Father some money, because this way it won't run us into debt. . . ."

Papa looked at her. "Now I'll owe your father the money, instead of Mose. Along with the balance of the money I owe him for Lady. And what it'll cost him to keep Lady there, and pay a vet. . . ."

"He doesn't have to pay the vet. The vet said if I'd have Lady do her tricks for his kids next weekend, he wouldn't charge anything. He liked her tricks, Papa. And Grandpa said he'd get the keep out of my hide when we go haying."

Papa gave him a long look, as if he had never really seen him before. Then he turned and walked out of the yard.

David didn't know whether to offer help or what. It seemed better just to keep his mouth shut. He was confused because Papa hadn't yelled at him. He looked at Mama. She was watching Papa as he walked down the road. Then she turned fiercely on David.

"How could you do that to him?"

David was astonished and hurt. Mama almost never was angry with him. "I didn't mean to. . . ."

"You deliberately disobeyed him. He's told you and told you to stay away from fires."

"But Mama. . . ."

"Now you've ruined Lady. Not to mention risking your own life. Now what is he going to do about the taxi? Tell me that. How is he going to manage now?"

"Mama, I was afraid Grandpa might be in danger."

Her eyes were scornful. "Since when did my father need to be rescued by a child?"

"I'm not a child, Mama."

"You're a child as long as you act like a child. You wanted to go to that fire, and you just used your grandfather as an excuse."

David wanted to answer her back but he couldn't because he knew what she said was true. He *had* used Grandpa as an excuse. "Well," he said lamely, "now Papa will get the auto and things will be better. . . ."

She made a furious gesture with her hand. "He doesn't want the auto. Why can't the man do things his own way? Why does everybody make it so hard for him. . . ." To David's horror she began to cry. She swept her apron over her face and ran into the house. In a few minutes he heard her playing the elaborate scale exercises that she gave her advanced pupils. She always said she did them to keep her fingers limber, but David noticed she did them when she was nervous or upset.

Unable to think of anything to do that wouldn't make things worse, David went up to his room. From his window he saw Papa come back with the livery horse, hitch him to the coach, and go off to the depot.

When David went out through the kitchen, on his way to

light the lamps, Mama smiled at him as if nothing had happened. He smelled the bubbling molasses in the pot of baked beans that she was slow-cooking, and he saw the brown-crusted gingerbread that she was taking out of the stove. Mama's cakes never failed.

Papa didn't come home for supper, at least not at the usual time. Mama put his plate on the back of the stove to keep warm. David tried to think of something to talk about, but he couldn't. He felt bad, partly because Mama had been cross with him, but mostly because he knew she was right.

Finally he said, "I know it doesn't do any good, but I'm awful sorry. I wish I knew what to do."

Mama looked sad. "So do I." That was all she said.

He took a piece of gingerbread with him and went out. More people than usual were out, standing in little knots talking about the fire, or wandering down the street as if the excitement hadn't worn off yet and they didn't know what to do with themselves.

Mrs. Pulsifer called to him from her front piazza, where she was rocking in her creaky wicker rocker, working away on a bag of chocolate-covered vanilla creams. He didn't want to talk to her, but he had to be polite. He went up the walk and stood on her steps. "Must have been a terrible fire, Davey."

"Yes, it was."

She held out the bag of candy and he took one. "I guess so. Terrible thing, both those icehouses. An awful loss. I saw you tearing off on Lady."

"Yes." David bit into the cream. He loved chocolate-covered vanilla creams, especially this kind that was sort of dry, not squashy and wet.

"I don't suppose your papa went."

"No, he didn't go." David took a cautious step backward, preparing to leave.

"He don't go to fires much, since that time up to the Giddings place." She rocked violently, making the chair creak. "I remember how he got hurt, poor man."

David had heard the story of his father's accident in bits and pieces since he was old enough to listen, and he had long ago stopped paying attention. Now he tried to remember about it.

"He was in such pain. Great big joist fell on his arm, pinned him right to the ground. Mr. Pulsifer told me all about it. Mr. Pulsifer was a great one for going to fires, 'fore he died."

David winced. With the memory of the icehouse fires vivid in his mind, he could imagine Papa hit by a falling joist, pinned to the ground. He had never really thought about it as something real happening. It must have hurt, all right.

"Well, you be careful, Davey. Don't you get hurt."

"I'll be careful."

"I used to worry something terrible about Mr. Pulsifer, scared he'd get himself hurt."

David took another step backward. "Thank you for the chocolate cream."

"Ayuh." She was looking past him, and David knew she was thinking about Mr. Pulsifer, who used to drive the coal cart and always looked as if somebody had shot his face full of cinders.

Passing the blacksmith shop he waved to Abel, who was working late, sparks flying up from the forge. Abel straightened up, mopped his forehead with his arm, and wiped his hands on his black leather apron. "Bad fire," he called.

"Awful bad." It made David feel important because everybody knew he'd gone to help fight the fire. It was only Papa who thought it was wrong.

He stopped in front of Bert Noah Story's place, where the Storys made wooden anchor windlasses, and peered through the window. But it was getting dark, and he couldn't see anything.

Pinky Callahan and Joel Marsh were hanging on the handlebars of their bikes in front of Claiborne's, and David joined them for a minute. Part of the beautiful wrought-iron fence that George Claiborne was making for the Henry Frick estate was visible through the window of the shop. Pinky and Joel wanted to know about the fire. They'd both been in Gloucester with their mothers and had missed the whole thing. They were angry and envious.

"What was it like?" Pinky asked.

David, remembering fires he hadn't been allowed to go to, knew how they felt. He tried to describe it, but how could you make anybody see it who wasn't there? He told about the flames and the scorching heat and the smoke that choked you, and the big smash when parts of the building fell down. But the more they listened, the unhappier they were. He left them muttering to themselves that it probably wasn't any better than any other fire.

A group of old men sat around the cold, pot-bellied stove in Mr. Perkins's store next to the post office, smoking and talking the way they always did. Remembering old fires, probably.

He went down to the yard, not knowing really where he

wanted to go, and stood looking up at the vessel they had just framed up, the *Minerva Four*. It was going to be a pleasure boat for some friend of the President's. President Taft had a summer place at Pride's Crossing, though he didn't get down there much now he was President of the country. They said there'd be a big to-do when the *Minerva Four* was launched, a lot of bigwigs from politics and all that. Some elegant lady from Boston or Washington, D.C., would probably break the bottle of champagne and fall in the river.

He patted the *Minerva* on her keel and wandered along the river. He picked up a discarded copy of the *Essex Echo* to swat at mosquitoes; they were fierce tonight. He stopped to look at the crazy little boat Andrew had made with a bicycle frame geared to a pair of paddles, so you could ride it like a bike. Andrew had made it out of scrap, and sold it to Jimmy Dooley for five dollars. Andrew was the only one in the family who knew how to make money.

He tried to walk lightly on the spongy bottom that was left at low tide. Once he sank into brackish water up to his ankles, but he grabbed at eel grass and got onto firmer ground. Without really planning it, he was making for the spar yard, where he and Andrew used to play a lot when they were younger. The masts, called "sticks," were stored in a tidal creek until they were needed.

It was dark when he got there, and out on the water the one-celled creatures called "light-of-the-night" set the water ablaze with light. Near him a pair of ducks were feeding on widgeon grass, and further up the creek a night heron was fishing.

When he came to the spar yard, he squatted down and put his ear to one end of a log. But it was no fun alone—there was nothing to hear. When Andrew was with him, Andrew had gone out to the other end of the log and scratched it very gently with his fingernail, and David had heard the sound perfectly. It had always seemed like some kind of magic.

If Andrew were here, he'd probably have bought the Ford by now, somehow or other, and be teaching Papa how to drive it. Some people could do just about anything, and some people couldn't. David scratched the end of a spar with his fingernail and quickly put his ear to it, but of course he couldn't hear anything because that wasn't the way it worked.

Off in the marsh he could see the small red light from some tramp's fire. He wondered if it was any fun to be a tramp. It seemed lonesome.

He took Grandma's silver thimble holder out of his pocket, opened it, and ran his thumb over the top of the steel fragment that killed Crazy Horse. He could almost hear Grandpa's voice, he'd told them the story so many times: "It was General George Crook, that the Indians called Three Stars, who sent his men out to bring in Crazy Horse, because Crazy Horse had warned the Indians not to scout for the white man. Three Stars had sent word to Crazy Horse that if he would surrender with his nine hundred men, Three Stars would give them a reservation. The Indians were starving, and Crazy Horse wanted to save them, but he soon knew he had been betrayed again. He was arrested, and boys, this is the saddest part: he was arrested by his old friend Little Big Man, who had once been so brave and had now been bought out by the white man. Crazy Horse saw the stinking jail they were leading him to. . . . I stood there not fifty yards away, boys; I saw it happen. . . . He lunged to get free and they plunged a bayonet into his gut. . . ." Grandpa always stopped here, as if it were too painful to remember. "He died that night. Thirty-five years old. A brave man, a good man." And Andrew always asked, "How did you get the bayonet, Grandpa?" "I paid the soldier two dollars for it, and I had the tip cut off. I gave the rifle to a museum in Washington, D.C. Thought it might do them good to look at it once in a while."

David sat looking down at the steel tip. A brave man, a good man. Life was a very hard thing. He put it back in his pocket, carefully, where it couldn't fall out, and got up to go home. The tide was coming in, black water filling up the black night. He moved to higher ground. He hoped Andrew was all right. For all they knew, he could be at the bottom of the sea. . . . David shivered. Only one postcard from Nova Scotia, a long time ago, and no word from the vessel since. Clinging to the coarse grass, he pulled himself up to the road and went home, the frogs harrumphing somewhere inland and the high-pitched hum of insects ringing in his ears.

12

Nothing terrible happened. Papa rented the livery-stable horse, and the week dragged by. The *Mildred W.* was going to be launched on Sunday. Papa went off to the tavern in Ipswich or down to Gloucester every now and again, but he didn't come home drunk. The weather was that kind of hot, breathless weather that makes you think something is going to happen, either good or bad.

David worked hard at the yard, helping the men get ready for the launching, and working on the *Minerva* too because she would be next. She was a rush job.

Somebody said that a woman down to Rockport had gotten word that Andrew's vessel was going to come home in a few weeks, but nobody seemed to know who the woman was or anything definite about it. Those rumors were always drifting around when a vessel had been gone a long time. Mama began counting the days it would take for the ship to get from the Banks to Gloucester, if it had a tail wind all the way. David tried not to think about it because if you thought about things too much, you were apt to be disappointed.

On the day before the launching, David went out on the road to watch Si Potter's team deliver lumber from the freight yard to the James yard. It was always a sight to see: a span of big, well-trained horses pulling the high-wheeled wagon with its load of seventy-foot-long planks that dragged in the dirt behind the wagon. They had to go down an incline from the road to the yard, and when Jake Johnson was driving, as he was today, they always did it without even slowing up; just lickety-split down that little dirt track to the yard.

When he was little, David used to think he'd like to drive a team like that, but now he was old enough to know that you could grow old in a job like that and never make enough to buy your own team.

Jake turned the big brown horses smartly and yelled "Giddap!" While the wagon was making the turn, he jumped off, still holding the reins, and ran alongside it.

"Look at that son-of-a-gun," Horace said. He was standing beside David, chewing on a boiled lobster claw. "He don't care what he does. It ain't his team."

But it was exciting to watch, just the same. Then as the tail of the wagon lurched up over the road and onto the narrow dirt track, David heard Horace gasp.

"Load's shifting!" Horace started across the street on a dead run. "Jake! Load's shifting!"

Jake had already noticed it, and he leaped onto the side of the wagon, trying to hold back the heavy lumber. David ran across the road to help, but there was nothing anyone could do. Jake jumped for the horses' heads to slow them

down, but they were going too fast. Slowly the big planks shifted forward until they were extended way out over the backs of the first pair of horses. David stood still, holding his breath. The planks inched forward until they were up to the horses' heads and still the horses didn't slow their pace down the incline to the yard.

"God a-mighty!" Horace said. "Them horses'll get their heads sheared off."

But because they hadn't slowed down, they reached the level ground before the lumber got that far. Slowly, slowly, the planks began to slide back again. Without any guidance from anyone, the horses trotted smartly along and stopped at the place where the lumber was always unloaded.

David heard Horace give a weak whistle, and behind them a crowd that had gathered to watch what had looked like a sure disaster sent up a cheer for the horses.

"They got better sense than we have," Horace said, "damned if they ain't."

When David told about it at supper, his father said, "Jake's telling it around town that he knew they could handle it. Says he's trained 'em so good, they can do anything. Says he never turned a hair."

David hooted. "I saw him. He was scared spitless."

"Well, mind you do as well, getting that vessel off the ways tomorrow."

After supper David went down to the yard for a last private look at the *Mildred W*. She sat high on the ways, looking ghostly in the moonlight. The drag, a bundle of big timbers held together with a chain, had already been fastened to the vessel with a hawser. When the boat went down the ways, the hawser that was coiled on the ground would pay out until finally the line would go taut, and the drag would snake along the ground, smashing anything that got in the way. The drag was like a brake that kept the boat from going down the ways too fast. One year David had seen a dory smashed to matchsticks by the drag after it started flailing along the shore. Launching was a tricky business; you had to look out for a lot of things.

He saw Papa go by. He hoped he'd stay sober; he had to meet a bunch of people from Boston tomorrow that were coming for the launching. Somebody said Mr. Henry Cabot Lodge was coming.

He looked up at the vessel, trying to imagine what kind of adventures she would have. Now that she was finished, she seemed almost a stranger to him, mysterious in the darkness, ready to start a life of her own. He put out his hand, reaching up to touch the keel. "Good luck, *Mildred W.*," he said. "Good voyage."

When he saw her again in the morning, she was decked out in bunting.

At noon Papa put on his best hat and drove the livery-stable rig out to meet the special train. The shipyard men worked through the dinner hour getting ready. By one o'clock a good-sized crowd had gathered. The vessel was due to be launched at one-fifteen. There were thunderclouds in the sky, and a smart wind from the east snapped the flags on the boat. Everybody kept looking anxiously downriver for the tugboat. Sometimes if the easterly wind was strong enough, it could prevent the tug from crossing the bar at the mouth of the river.

Kids with firecrackers were bothering the foreman. He kept driving them away from the yard. "They could start a fire," he said, kicking at a pile of dry shavings, "or make the carpenters nervous." Finally Pete Alzar caught the oldest Floyd boy by the arm and talked to him quietly for a few minutes. After that the boys stopped setting off the firecrackers in the yard, although you could still hear them popping along the road.

David felt tense, the way he always did before a launching. There was something exciting about it, not just the crowds, and the town band that was playing away in the wind, but the fact that a vessel had been put together right here in Essex, by men he knew, and at least a little bit this time with his own help.

He felt relieved when he saw the coach pull up, Papa sitting very straight. The men looked important, although somebody said Mr. Lodge hadn't come after all. They were mostly stout men, in white linen suits and hard straw hats, and three of them held furled umbrellas. There were several ladies too, one in a long, pale-green dress and a little shawl around her shoulders and a white leghorn hat. She'd be the one, David supposed, who would smash the bottle of champagne.

One of the men made a speech, but David couldn't hear him, with the wind blowing the other way. It didn't make any difference; they always said the same old things.

The team of carpenters stood on either side of the big sledlike device that the hull of the vessel rested on. The tracks of the sled, called the ground ways, were bolted to the sliding ways, which looked like the runners of the sled. Two pairs of carpenters stood at the upper ends of the two sliding ways, each pair with a crosscut saw, ready to saw off the sliding ways so the vessel could slip down into the river. They had to work in perfect unison or the boat might topple over. David remembered once when he was a little boy a boat at the James and Tarr yard had fallen over that way.

He could see the sweat on the face of Harry Duke, the carpenter nearest him, who stood with his hands on the saw and his feet braced. They couldn't start, though, till the tugboat was sighted, because if they did, they might have to let the vessel float free right there in the river, getting into all kinds of trouble, smashed up probably, with the wind blowing the way it was.

The crowd stood waiting, and the band struggled with a military march that was meant to spruce everybody up. All eyes were on the river, watching for the tug. Suddenly at their backs there was an explosive chugging and a blast on a horn. Everybody jumped and whirled around to see what on earth it was.

David saw Papa break out of the crowd and run into the street. The horn blew again, and through a hole in the crowd David saw Uncle Tom, driving the crazy machine that was made out of two Fords. Aunt Eloise sat up beside him, big as billy, wearing one of those long veils wound around her hat. People began to laugh, and David felt humiliated. Uncle Tom ought to know better than to interrupt a launching that way. He could see Papa talking to him, and Papa looked mad. For once he knew how he felt. Uncle Tom had made fools of them.

"What is that damned-fool thing?" a man behind David said.

Another man laughed. "Looks like a couple of mating

crabs. Ain't that Tom O'Brien? Hey, Davey, ain't that your Uncle Tom?"

"Yes," David said. He felt ashamed.

The man laughed again. "What's that thing he's driving?"

"Somebody put two Fords together."

"What's it good for?"

"He wants to use it for a taxi."

"Hey!" said the first man. "That's a smart idea!"

"Leave it to Tom," said the second man. "He's full of smart ideas. Got the old touch; everything turns to gold."

David was confused. Should he be ashamed of Uncle Tom or proud of him? But he was saved the trouble of deciding. Somebody screamed, "Towboat's comin'!" And everybody forgot about Uncle Tom.

As the crowd gathered again close to the vessel, a hush fell over them. The foreman lifted his hand and everybody tensed.

The foreman's voice rose, words clear above the wind. "Ready! Stop at your first mark!"

The four carpenters sawed at the ways. The ladies in the crowd shivered and pulled up their collars as the wind whipped through the yard. The foreman glanced quickly at the clouds and back again to the men. The first blocks fell to the ground.

"Take your second mark! Saw away!"

Only the wind and the sound of the saws and the screech of the gulls could be heard. The tugboat moved up the river and idled offshore.

The vessel inched her way toward the river.

"Take your mark! Saw away!"

The *Mildred W.* gave a loud crack and a groan.

"She's on her way!"

The woman in green swung out wildly with the bottle of champagne and missed. She swung again, just in time. The neck broke off the bottle and a tiny shower of champagne flew into the air, but the bottle fell into the river. Teddy Akins dove in with all his clothes on and came up holding it high. Everybody cheered.

The *Mildred W.* slid down the ways, gathering speed as she went. As her stern dipped into the water it made a big splash, and the tugboat gave a hoot. The crowd yelled. But something was wrong. The cheers changed to a low moan as the vessel, instead of lifting into the river, stuck with her stern in the mud. The foreman ran into the river, right up to his shoulders in water, almost as if he thought he could push her free. The towboat fastened on and tried to pull her. People were running around. The lady in the green dress pulled her skirts up and ran right down to the edge of the river. It was beginning to rain, but she paid no attention.

"Can't they do something?" she wailed. "What happened?"

"It's her husband's vessel," somebody said.

"Lady," another man said, "they'll get her off. The tide's still coming in."

"But how could it happen?" Her hat was askew, and raindrops that looked like tears streaked her face.

"Mud silts up. You never can be sure."

The onlookers began to thin out as the rain came down

harder. The people from Boston opened their umbrellas and waited. They had planned to ride her down to Gloucester.

Some people went over to look at Uncle Tom's Ford. David saw Papa still there, and Harvey Milliken, all three of them talking hard, Mr. Milliken with his arms around the shoulders of Papa and Uncle Tom, like a coach with a couple of ball players.

For about half an hour the men watched, in the steady rain, while the tugboat pulled at the hawser. Finally she floated free, and somebody sent David running down to the restaurant to tell the Boston people she was afloat.

Almost everybody else had gone home when the *Mildred W.* was brought about so the Boston people could board her for the ride down around Cape Ann. Sometimes, on a good day, some of the kids went along, and grown-ups too, with a picnic hamper, and afterward they'd come home on the electrics. But today the weather kept them home.

David stayed with the other yardmen, watching, until the vessel set off behind the towboat down the river.

"Just as glad I ain't going around the Cape on a day like this," Horace said.

Pete looked down at David. "You better get home, youngster, and get out of them soaking-wet clothes before you catch your never-get-over."

When David came into the house, Papa and Mama and Uncle Tom and Aunt Eloise were in the kitchen drinking coffee. David could tell the men's coffee was spiked because Papa's jug of rum was on the table. They seemed happy.

"Hurry up, boy," Uncle Tom said, "we've been waiting for you."

"Davey, give yourself a good rubdown and get into some dry clothes," Mama said. "You'll catch a cold."

"Make it snappy," Uncle Tom said. "We're all ready to go."

"Go where?"

"Uncle Tom is taking us to Gloucester for a shore dinner," Mama said.

"In the rain?"

"Listen, lad," Uncle Tom said, "listen to me, nephew, that elegant vehicle you see outside has a handmade, guaranteed, surefire, keep-out-the-weather top. Now you hustle."

"I have to light the lamps."

"Your father got Danny to do it," Mama said.

David was puzzled. Papa didn't hold with getting Danny to do the lights; he only let David get him when David was really sick. He looked at his father. "What's up?"

His father took a playful swipe at him. "Hurry up! I'm hungry!"

David dried himself off and dressed as fast as he could. Why worry about reasons? A ride to Gloucester in the Ford and a shore dinner were all anybody could want.

13

David wished it were a good day so people would be out on the street when the strange Ford drove past Stage Fort Park along the rocky shore. He'd have liked to have everybody see this machine he was riding in, right up front beside Uncle Tom.

After he parked in front of the tavern, Uncle Tom put rocks in front of the wheels. "No sense taking chances," he told Papa.

They were almost the only people in the tavern. Uncle Tom ordered for everybody, the complete shore dinner, with clams on the half-shell and fried sole, and baked stuffed lobsters, baked potatoes, steamed clams, Indian pudding.

"Oh my," Mama said. "I've never seen so much food."

"There's nothing like a good shore dinner," Aunt Eloise said.

Uncle Tom ceremoniously poured wine into two small wine glasses for the ladies. "For you and me, brother

Nathan. . . ." He filled their water tumblers half-full. "Is David old enough for a wee drap of the stuff that cheers?"

"No," Papa said. His cheerfulness had disappeared, and he seemed moody. He enjoyed his clams on the half-shell, but then he sat with his chin on his hand staring at the rain that slashed across the window, and beyond, into the harbor. "It's been about ten thousand years," he said, "since the Ice Age did its damndest to grind this cape to dust."

"And here we still are," Mama said.

He looked at Uncle Tom suddenly, almost accusingly. "We could get another ice age, you know."

Uncle Tom wiped the ketchup from his chin. "Not in my time."

"Oh, Nathan," Aunt Eloise said, "let's think about cheerful things."

"Well," Papa said, "I imagine there are those things that find an ice age a cheerful prospect." He grinned suddenly. "A chunk of ice, for instance."

"I knew Harvey would come around," Uncle Tom said. He raised his glass. "Let's drink to Harvey. Drink to Nathan's success."

Papa looked at David, who was pausing with a steamed clam half way to his mouth. "Don't sit there looking half-witted, child," he said. "In case nobody's told you, Harvey Milliken and I have gone partners with your uncle's Ford."

David gasped. He put down the clam, dripping melted butter on the white tablecloth. Mama leaned over and mopped it up with her napkin. "You mean you're going to have the machine for a taxi?"

"That seems to be the gist of it."

"Hey!" David said, more loudly than he meant to. "Hey! That is *great!*"

Even Papa laughed.

"Can I learn how to drive it?"

"I've got to learn myself first."

"It won't take more'n half an hour, Nathan," Uncle Tom said. "Nothing to it."

Papa shook his head, but all he said was, "Look at that lobster!"

The waiter set huge plates of baked stuffed lobster in front of each of them, and brought the big shell-crackers and the picks to get the meat out of the claws. Lobster was David's favorite food, and he tried to think about it, but he couldn't get his mind off the auto.

Just as Papa cracked the big claw, a clap of thunder seemed to smash against the rocks below them. The surf was pounding on the rocks, shooting up clouds of spray.

"I hope they got the vessel to Gloucester safely," Mama said.

"They'll have gone through the cut," Papa said. "They're probably there by now."

After dinner Uncle Tom drove them to Rockport to see the surf. He left the auto in town and they walked out on Bearskin Neck, past the fishermen's shacks, the bait shops, the saloons, the Sea Fencibles Barracks, where the militia had stayed that defended the point from the British in the War of 1812. They had to lean into the wind, and after a few minutes Aunt Eloise went back to the auto.

"Must be a forty-miler," Papa said. He held Mama's arm.

Nobody was in sight except the harbor master, who was

checking on the lobster boats down below them. Far out, almost too far to see, a thin line of white water spread like cream along the old, unfinished breakwater. The gray-black waves smashed against Bearskin Neck. David felt the saltwater on his face and tasted it with his tongue on his lips. The wind screamed, and the gulls were flung about like scraps of paper. Holding to a chunk of granite, David leaned out, and was slammed in the face by a wave. Papa caught his arm.

"Careful."

The harbor master climbed up the wet rocks and nodded to them.

"Quite a storm," Papa said.

"She's a corker."

"Can we give you a hand with the boats?"

"No, thanks, everything seems to be shipshape." The man's oilskins streamed with water.

"Do you know if that vessel they launched in Essex made it down all right?"

"Yes, she made it in good shape. Hear she had a bit of trouble up there."

"Just a mite."

The harbor master nodded politely to Mama. "Nice to have seen you folks."

Uncle Tom joined him as he walked back up the narrow street.

"Time to go," Papa said.

But Mama seemed reluctant to leave. She was staring out at the sea, her eyes narrowed against the rain, and David knew she was thinking about Andrew. Finally she turned to him and, her voice almost inaudible over the wind, she said, "Don't go to sea, Davey."

He took her hand. "I won't, Mama. I don't even want to."

As they walked up the muddy street, he wondered what he did want. He was going to have to decide pretty soon.

The homemade side curtains that the original owner had put up began to flap loose on the ride home, and the rain poured in on them. Uncle Tom flattened down the windshield, which divided in the middle, because he couldn't see through the rain-streaked glass, so the rain drove at them from the front too. Aunt Eloise wasn't happy, but David was. He kept thinking, "This is our Model T! Our own Ford!"

The dirt road had become a sea of mud, and three times David and his father had to get out and push, while Uncle Tom steered and yelled directions.

"I must be out of my mind," Papa said, as he leaned into the rear wheels. "Never had to push a horse out of the mud."

"But a carriage can get stuck, Papa," David said.

Papa muttered something David couldn't hear.

When they reached the Essex town limits, the rain suddenly stopped, and the last pale light of the setting sun shone in the puddles.

Mama heated big kettles of water so everybody could take the chill out of his bones, and while the others were bathing and changing clothes, she made coffee and warmed up the salt-fish hash left from breakfast. Uncle Tom and Aunt Eloise were staying all night.

"We'll be your papa's first customers," Uncle Tom said to David, when he came down to the kitchen, pink-cheeked and dry. "We'll take the train to Hamilton, and Amory will meet us in *my* auto. Two Fords in the family. What do you think about that, Davey?"

David thought it was almost too wonderful to be believed.

When they had eaten, Uncle Tom took Papa out and taught him to drive. First they went up and down the yard, and then out toward the road. David longed to go, but Papa didn't want anyone watching him. He could hear the chickens squawk with terror as Papa drove the Ford pell-mell through the yard.

"I can't bear to look," Mama said.

From the window David saw Uncle Tom's face, teeth clenched, as the Ford lurched past the house. Brakes screeched. "Whew," David said. "He got out onto the street, Mama. He's doing fine."

While they were gone, he studied the diagram of the Ford that Uncle Tom had left in the house. It had so many parts, David didn't think he could ever learn what they all were called, let alone what they did. Magneto coils, drain cocks, intake pipe, cam shaft, carburetor. . . . He pored over it all until his eyes ached in the smoky light of the kerosene lamp. Gradually he began to make some sense out of it. If he could get the hood up and study it firsthand. . . .

"David," Mama said, "you'd better get to bed."

He took the diagram to bed with him and studied it some more by candlelight, till he was too sleepy to hold his head up any longer.

14

The next noon David went home to see if everything had gone all right with the auto. He found Papa with the hood up, staring into the engine.

"Anything wrong, Papa?"

"No, I'm just trying to figure 'er out. Tried to crank her up a little while ago, and it took me ten or fifteen minutes."

David climbed into the driver's seat. "Try it now."

Papa cranked but nothing happened.

"Try 'er again."

This time the engine roared into life. Papa straightened up. "What'd you do?"

"Advanced the spark."

Papa came around and looked. "That's right. Tom told me that. I forgot it. The thing's got so damned many parts."

With the engine running, David got out and looked under the hood.

"Now what do you suppose that durned thing is?" Papa said, pointing.

"That's the spark plug."

Papa looked at him skeptically. "How'd you know that?"

"I looked at that chart Uncle Tom left."

"So did I, and I might as well try to read Greek. What's this thing here?"

"Combustion chamber."

"I wonder if the Lord equipped your generation with some kind of knowledge of all this stuff, that he didn't give to us."

David laughed. "It's just that I like it."

"I better take you out tonight and let you drive her. The more of us knows how, the better off we are."

"Can I take it down the yard now?"

"Might as well. Try not to kill the chickens. Do you know what to do with your feet?"

"Yes, I watched Uncle Tom."

"Fire away, then." Papa climbed into the passenger seat. "That stick on the wheel is your gas."

"I know it." David pushed the clutch pedal in and cautiously pulled down the throttle lever. The Ford jumped ahead quicker than he had expected. He shoved down the brake pedal, and they shuddered to a stop.

Papa laughed, putting out a hand to brace himself against the windshield. "I'm glad you haven't got it down cold. That would have given me a terrible jolt."

"I only know a little bit from watching. Mr. James let me look at his, but that's not a Ford—it's different. Can I go around the yard again?"

"Batten your hatches."

At first David couldn't drive it without jerking and stalling and having to get out and crank again. Papa couldn't

crank it with his bad right hand, so he was trying to learn to use his left.

"Wish I could just say giddap to the damned thing," he said.

David was so engrossed in getting the hang of driving the auto that he forgot about the time until he heard the church bell ringing out the back-to-work time. He stopped the auto with a jerk and jumped out. "I'm late!"

"Run, Davey."

He ran all the way to the shipyard, but no one seemed to notice that he was late. Because he hadn't taken time to eat his dinner, he ached with hunger all afternoon.

Mama gave him a sandwich to take with him when he went out to light the lamps. "I hope the machine is working all right," she said. "Your father's a little late."

When David lighted the last lamp on his route, he noticed Old Harry, the scissors grinder, going into the Pace yard with a handful of knives he'd sharpened for them. He nodded to David and gave him his strange toothless smile. When David was a little boy, he'd thought Old Harry was possibly the devil. But he knew now that the man was harmless. He lived alone in a filthy little shack in the woods, and he cooked his meals on an open fire. People said he'd been a Gypsy once and the tribe had thrown him out, but David doubted it. Sometimes boys went up to the shack and looked for buried treasure; old Harry made a pretty good living with his ancient grindstone, and no one knew what he did with the money. Papa said it was nobody's business.

David stopped to look at the ancient horse that pulled the little rig. The horse was lame and half-blind, although Old Harry still put blinders on him as if he were a perky young horse that might bolt. He stood with his head hanging down, his mane matted and tangled. "Poor old horse," David said. "I wish I had an apple for you." He thought of Lady. Over the Fourth he'd go up to Grandpa's and see her. Maybe Papa would drive them up in the machine so Grandpa could admire it. But then he remembered that Grandpa didn't like automobiles. It was hard to imagine an intelligent man like Grandpa not liking automobiles.

As David came to the corner of his own street, he heard the taxi coming. Grinning with pleasure, he waited to see it go by. Mr. Milliken was sitting up front with Papa, waving to David. Papa gave David a quick glance, but he didn't risk a wave. He drove with his back pushed against the seat and his arms held out straight and rigid in front of him, as if he were trying to control a boat in a heavy storm. He drove so slowly, the Ford kept bucking.

David watched them go down the road. Just after they passed Old Harry's rig, the Ford backfired. The terrified horse reared and neighed, made a wide circle in the street that almost upset the rig, and galloped in the opposite direction, toward David. Blind and unsteady, the horse veered toward an elm, almost hit it, and plunged back into the street. His head was up, and his eyes rolled wildly.

David crouched, trying to find a way to stop him. The reins flapped on the horse's back, half-tangled up in the shafts of the flimsy rig. He'd have to leap for the bridle. He could hear Old Harry yelling, running up the street, and he heard Papa call to him. The thunder of the horse's hooves drowned out words. A runaway horse was a scary thing because you never knew what a horse would do in panic, especially a poor old horse that could hardly see.

David yelled, "Whoa!" and jumped for the bridle. For a second he had his fingers on it, but the horse plunged sideways, throwing David off. He fell into the dust as the horse thundered past him. Old Harry ran by him, shaking his fist and yelling. Then there was a rending crash and the noise of the hooves stopped.

For an instant David was too horrified to move. Then he ran up the street, passing Old Harry. The horse had run into a lamp post at the turn in the road. The rig was in splinters, and the horse lay on his side, dead.

15

Papa and Old Harry had been talking out on the back step for a long time. Old Harry, in his wheedling, whiny voice, kept saying he would have to sue Papa if Papa didn't buy him a new horse and rig, and Papa kept saying it would take a while, he didn't have the money.

"I'll make it good to you, Harry," Papa said. "I'm a man of my word."

"And in the meantime, in the meantime I starve, hey?"

David sat in the kitchen with Mama. "He won't starve," he muttered. "The old miser."

"Shh," Mama said. "Your father feels responsible."

"But he couldn't help it if the auto backfired."

"It's his auto; he feels responsible."

"You got that fancy automo-*beel*," Old Harry kept saying. "You must be a rich man."

And again Papa, who hated to tell his private business, would explain to Old Harry the financial arrangement under which he had the taxi.

"Just the same, a man with an automo-*beel* like that, he's a rich man. I'm just a poor man. I work sunrise to sunset to keep outa the poorhouse."

David snorted. Everybody knew Old Harry only worked when he felt like it.

Mama looked as if she felt like crying. "Your father said an automobile would bring trouble. Here it is already."

"It's not the auto, it's that trouble-making old fool."

"But his horse was killed, Davey."

"That poor horse is better off dead. He never treated it right. I've seen him flog it just because it wasn't moving fast enough to please him."

Papa spoke again. "The only thing I can do, Harry, is repair the gig myself; I can do that."

"And I pull it myself, like an old nag, eh?"

"No, I'll give you my own horse."

David felt as if he were going to faint. "Mama," he said, "Mama, stop him. . . ."

"She's an old horse," Papa was saying, "and she can't pull much of a load any more. Got trouble with her legs. But she could handle that light little gig of yours."

David got up, but Mama reached out and grabbed his arm.

"Well," Old Harry said, as if he were thinking over a bad bargain, "that old nag of yours, she ain't worth more than six, seven dollars."

"She's worth at least ten," Papa said. There was a note of annoyance in his voice now. He hated to haggle. "She's worth three times what your poor old blind horse was worth.

I'll give you the horse, worth at least ten dollars, and I'll mend the rig for you. You'll be better off than you were before."

Harry's whiny voice hung on his words. "We . . e . . ll, when do I get this here horse? She ain't here now."

"My boy will get her for you over the Fourth."

"I'll lose almost a week's work."

"It won't be the first time, Harry."

"I'll have to think it over, Mr. O'Brien. I might come out better to take you to court."

"Take it or leave it right now, Harry. Do you want to settle for the horse or not?"

"And you'll repair the rig?"

"Yes."

"We . . e . . ll. . . . I ought to see me a lawyer. . . ."

"Take it or leave it."

"All right, I'll take it. You have the horse for me after the Fourth?"

"You'll have it a week from today."

David heard the creak of the step as Papa stood up.

"Good evening, Harry."

" 'Evening, Mr. O'Brien. I can trust your word?"

Papa's voice was cold. "I hope you know that."

"Yeah, well, some people . . . you know how it is. . . ."

Papa came into the kitchen. His face was pale and stiff, as if he had been controlling himself at great cost. He hardly glanced at David and Mama. David heard Old Harry's off-key whistling as he trudged down the yard.

"Papa, you can't do that with Lady."

Papa turned on him so furiously, David ducked, thinking

he was going to hit him. "Don't you try to tell me what I can and can't do."

"Papa, Old Harry mistreats horses. He'll kill her."

"I have no choice. The accident occurred because of me, and I have no money to pay damages. Go to your room, David. And remember, have that horse back here by next Monday morning."

David took a deep breath. "I won't do it, Papa."

Mama gasped, but she didn't say anything.

Papa's face darkened. "Are you refusing to obey me?"

"I'm sorry, Papa, I can't turn Lady over to that old devil."

Papa glared at him a moment and then turned to Mama. "Ring up your father and tell him we're coming for the horse Sunday."

"No," David said. "Don't do that."

"You have your choice. You bring her, or we go get her."

David looked at the floor. "I'll go."

"Very well." Papa got his hat and started out of the house.

"Will you be gone long?" Mama asked anxiously.

"I haven't the slightest idea." He went out of the yard on foot.

"David," Mama said, "We can keep an eye on Lady. If that man mistreats her, we can report him. . . ."

"He's not going to get her," David said.

She looked frightened. "David, you must do what your father says."

"Not if he's wrong."

"It seems wrong to you because you love Lady, but your father feels responsible to that man."

"Well, let him. I don't." Disregarding his mother's face, he stomped upstairs to his room and went to bed. When she looked in on him later, he pretended to be asleep. He lay awake a long time, thinking. He was going to save Lady but he hadn't yet figured out how to do it. He'd think of something, though. Lady wasn't going to be the slave of that old filthy, mean man, not even if David had to take her and run away from home.

16

On Saturday morning David was up before daylight. He had sought out Danny the night before, and, without asking anyone at home, he had arranged with Danny to take care of the lamps Saturday night. "I'm going up to my grandfather's. I think I'll stay up there the two days."

He took the bike and pedaled fast over the roads to Hamilton. He had the feeling, in the shadowy light of dawn, that Old Harry was right behind him, trying to get to Lady before he could. He rode the bike so fast, he was panting for breath when he came to the lake. He stopped for a minute, looking at the charred ruins of the icehouses, bleak in the early morning light. He wondered if they would be rebuilt. It took a lot of courage to rebuild something big like that, when it had been ruined through no fault of your own.

Mama would be getting up about now, and she'd find the note he'd left, telling her he was going to stay all night at Grandpa's. He had wanted to make sure Papa knew he was there so he wouldn't come after Lady himself.

Papa wouldn't be up yet, he thought, with a touch of scorn. When Papa came home the night before, he had been unsteady on his feet and his eyes had had that familiar, wild look. David and Mama had helped him upstairs, and he'd fallen back on the bed with a groan, his eyes shut. Then when Mama was pulling the blanket over him and David had taken off his shoes, Papa opened his bloodshot eyes and looked at Mama. He pointed his long finger at her and said, " 'I could not love thee half so well, Loved I not honor more.' " And then his head had fallen back on the pillow.

Downstairs David said, "Was that from the Bible, what Papa said?"

"No," Mama said, stroking her hair back with her hands, "no, it wasn't from the Bible. It was from a poem that I always thought was very silly."

"I didn't know Papa read poetry."

"Your father reads whatever happens to be within reach, whether it's a catalogue or *King Lear*. And I don't know that it helps him any."

David was still thinking about what Papa had said. "What did he mean, about honor?"

She looked at him. "You'll have to ask him. Honor is a word that men seem to feel they know a good deal about. I've never understood the word too well myself." She turned away and took the lid off the stove to see if the fire had burned down. "Sometimes I think it means false pride, but I'm only a woman; what do I know?"

David knew she was being sarcastic. She thought that

women were just as good as men, and she said so every now and then. "Maybe better in some ways," she'd say, "because there are differences, after all."

David pedaled the bike along the road toward Grandpa's, thinking about Mama and Papa. He knew they loved each other, but sometimes Mama must get awfully exasperated with Papa. Especially when he tried to run away from things by drinking too much or botching things. And yet she didn't seem to. He knew Papa felt bad about giving Lady to Old Harry; as soon as he'd gotten over being so awfully angry, he'd realized that. It was just that Papa couldn't see any way out of it. But there was going to be a way out. David intended to find one.

When he got to Grandpa's, he went first to the barn to see Lady, but she wasn't there. He spied her out in the field, and at the same moment she saw him. After a moment of hesitation, she came trotting toward him, and he noticed with mixed feelings of relief and worry that she wasn't limping. Papa would say she was able to pull Old Harry's rig.

He grabbed her around the neck and pulled on her forelock. "Lady! I missed you. How you been? You look great. You like it here; I can tell." She nickered and thrust her nose into his pocket. He laughed. "Still the same greedy old Lady. I didn't bring anything, but you've got this whole big field to find good things in. How you gettin' along with Pegasus?"

Pegasus was down at the far end of the field, his head hung over the stone wall, watching the world go by.

David rubbed Lady's ears. "Listen, I'll be right back. I'm going to go over to the polo field and make a little money. I'll take you with me, all right?"

Whenever he could, he went to the Myopia Hunt Club on days when there were polo games. He could always get a job walking the horses that weren't playing at the moment. He only made fifty cents a day, but he enjoyed the work, and he got to see part of the polo games.

He ran back to the house and found Grandpa cooking steak and fried potatoes for breakfast.

"Glad to see you, David. I thought you might come. You going to the Myopia?"

"Yes. I thought I'd ride Lady over. She looks fine, Grandpa."

"Well, we all benefit by a little rest and sunshine when we get old. The vet's children will be over there; he told me to tell you if you brought Lady over, she could do her tricks for them over there."

"All right. Sure." David found that he was very hungry. He'd been so worried for the last couple of days, he'd hardly eaten, but now, seeing Lady looking so well, he almost forgot the problem. But when he'd finished eating, he put down his fork and said, "Grandpa, what do you think about honor?"

Grandpa looked at him seriously for a moment. "Well, by and large, I guess I'm for it."

"What is it, anyway? I mean what is it exactly?"

Grandpa lighted his thin Cuban cigar and puffed out a small cloud of smoke. "Remember I was telling you last year, up to Parker River, that you've got to look out for certain words? Words that sound awful good but they may be booby-trapped. People use them to get you to do something you may not really think is right. Honor is one of those words."

"But what is it?"

Grandpa was silent for several minutes. "Not an easy question, Davey. Maybe it's doing what seems in your own heart to be right, not just what people will praise you for. A man may do what he feels his honor compels him to do, and still have other people defame him, even kill him. Jesus was an honorable man. So was Socrates. And they were killed for it. General Robert E. Lee was an honorable man, though I did not see things his way. Honor is a very private matter. It's not the shouts of praise from the multitude, and it's not false pride. In Louisiana and other places, men duel, kill each other over what they call affairs of honor. In my opinion that is simply pride."

"That's what Mama said, about false pride."

Grandpa smiled. "She's my daughter." He studied David a minute. "Something's on your mind, Davey. Do you want to tell me about it?"

David shook his head. "Not now, Grandpa. Later. I've got to do some thinking."

Grandpa nodded. "A wise decision. Always think first, if you can find the time."

"I guess I'd better get over to the Club." David got up and went out to get Lady. He could see Grandpa watching them way down the road until they were out of sight.

17

When David got there, carriages and buggies and a few automobiles already lined the curving drive that led to the Myopia Hunt Club. In the paddock in back of the stable, polo ponies nervously pawed the ground or moved around restlessly.

The big yellow-and-black coach with the fringed top, which belonged to the Club, was in front of the stable door. Patrick, the jaunty little Irishman who was the coachman, stood, arms akimbo, surveying the scene with his usual aloofness. David liked to be in Hamilton when Patrick, perched high on the driver's seat, wearing his livery and his top hat, drove the sleek horses at a smart trot down to the depot, to meet the men who stayed at the Club. It was a sight to see. The "summer people," who had town houses in Boston in the winter and who came to Hamilton, either to the Club or to the big estates they had built, in the summer, had given the town an air that Grandpa said was like an English countryseat. They played polo and rode to the hounds and rode in steeplechases and horse shows. It was a very different world from Essex.

David rode into the big stable, looking for his friend Jack Thompson, the head groom. It was Jack who always found David a job with one of the polo players. He found him out in back, currying a horse.

"Davey!" Jack said. "I haven't seen you in a month of Sundays. Where you been?"

"I'm working in the shipyard. I work six days a week."

Jack slapped the horse on the flank to make him turn. "Well, now. Building boats, are you? That's a grand thing. Say, if I'd a-known you were coming, I could have got you a job walking Mr. Prince's ponies. But I guess walking horses don't interest a big boat builder like you." He grinned at David.

"Sure, I'd like a job. Aren't there any left?"

"Not a one, lad. Not a one. But tomorrow now, it's the Horse Show, you know. I can get you something tomorrow."

Someone called to Jack.

"All right," David said. "I'll be here crack of dawn."

"You do that, lad."

David rode Lady over to the polo field. He was disappointed not to have a job, but at least there'd be tomorrow. He pulled her up behind the row of carriages that were lined up along the field. People were sitting in them, waiting for the game to start. Little kids balanced on the low, whitewashed boards that marked the boundaries of the field. David remembered how uncomfortable it was to sit on those thin pieces of wood.

He watched the first game. Polo was exciting, and these

players were so skilled, they could turn their horses on a dime. The horses themselves seemed to enjoy it, darting in toward the white wooden ball, stopping and turning and darting again with unbelievable speed and accuracy. The colorful helmets of the players and their silks and their white, stiffed-out riding pants, made a picture David liked to look at.

But after a while the warm sun made him sleepy. He turned Lady and rode her back a little way to the open pavilion where some of the children were playing. He slid off Lady's back and lay down in the warm grass, half-asleep, half-listening to the chatter of the children and the repeated whack of wooden mallets on wooden ball.

Somebody rumpled his hair. He looked up sleepily and saw the oldest daughter of Dr. Crane, the vet.

"Wake up," she said. "You're supposed to have your horse do us some tricks."

He rolled over. "Yeah. All right. Where are the other kids?"

"I'll get 'em." She ran around back of the pavilion, calling her sisters.

"Wake up, Lady. You got to put on your act." David took her around to the side of the pavilion. A plump, middle-aged nanny was dozing over a magazine, waking up abruptly whenever the small children in her charge wandered too far. She smiled at David.

In a minute David was surrounded by small children. "Hey," he said, "you aren't all Cranes, are you?"

"They're our friends," the oldest girl said.

"All right." He touched Lady lightly on her forehead, and she went up on her hind legs, waving her front feet in a pawing motion. In that position she turned around and around, bobbing her head up and down as she turned. The children squealed with delight, and the nanny had put her magazine aside, her face wreathed in smiles.

David put out his hand again, and Lady brought her front feet down, pawing the ground and ducking her head. As the children clapped, she weaved from side to side, bowing and bowing. David grinned. She was having a wonderful time. It had been a long time since she'd had such a good audience. He jumped on her back, his feet braced on either end of the saddle, his arms outspread to keep himself from falling. Lady trotted in a circle, keeping such a perfectly smooth gait, he didn't even waver, although it had been a long time since he had tried this stunt.

For about twenty minutes he kept Lady going through her tricks, and the crowd increased, including some adults. At last, when it seemed to him she had begun to favor her front leg a little, he brought her up on her hind legs and then down on her knees for her final bow. He swept his own arm over his heart in the elaborate gesture of the circus performer and bowed low. There was a loud sprinkle of applause and the children kept calling, "More!"

"No more today," David said. "I don't want her to get tired."

An old man in a white suit stood just beyond the circle of children, smiling, leaning with both hands on a silver-headed cane. When the children quieted down, he came over to David and put his hand on Lady's muzzle. "That's a nice little mare."

"Thank you," David said.

"It was nice of you to have her perform for the children."

"Well, I owed it to the Crane kids. Dr. Crane took care of Lady's leg free, if I would show the kids her tricks."

The old man bent down. "What's wrong with her leg?"

David explained to him the trouble Lady had had.

The old man nodded. "Age. It comes to us all." He took a small leather purse out of his coat pocket and took out a coin. "I enjoyed your little show myself."

David saw that the coin was a five-dollar gold piece. It was hard to keep from reaching out for it. It took him almost a week to earn that much. "No, thank you. I owed the show to the Crane kids. I'm glad you liked it too."

The old man studied him. "Will you be here for the horse show tomorrow?"

"Yes, I think so."

"Will you have your little mare do her tricks again for my grandchildren? If her leg is all right, of course. We don't want her to stiffen up."

"I'd be glad to."

"What's your name, young man?" When David told him, he said, "I think I know your grandfather. Tell him John Plummer sent his regards." He nodded and turned away.

David went back to the stable to talk to Jack Thompson. Jack was pitching hay from the loft into the stalls. David sat on an overturned pail and told Jack what had just happened.

"That would be Mr. Plummer. He was a great horseman in his day. Did something or other in the diplomatic service under President Roosevelt. Very nice man."

"Should I have taken the money?"

Jack leaned on the pitchfork, his eyes squinting. The stable smelled of horses and hay; sunlight streamed in through the wide doors. "No," he said, "it would have been all right to, but he probably liked you the better for saying no. Showed you was a gentleman. He'll make it up to you some way."

Although he hadn't meant to talk about it to anyone, David found himself telling Jack all about the Ford and the accident and Papa's having promised Lady to Old Harry. Jack went about his work as he listened, finishing up with the hay, filling pails of water, hosing down the dirt floor. He didn't speak until David was all through.

He shook his head. "I know that thievin' old scissors man. Hangs around here a lot. He don't take care of his horses."

"I know it," David said. "He beats them." Now that Jack had agreed with David's own view of Old Harry, it came to him very strongly that he simply could not take Lady back to Essex, no matter what happened. "I think I'll have to take her and go away," he said. "I can get a job someplace and just keep her where she can be nice and quiet." He hesitated. "You don't need a stable boy, do you, Jack?"

Jack sat down beside him. "No, I wish I did, and that's a fact. But Davey, if you was this close to home, your pa would find you and cart you off to Essex first thing."

"That's right. I'll have to go a long way." He felt faint, as if he hadn't eaten anything for a long time. "Maybe I could get a job up at the navy yard. . . ."

"I'll tell you what you do." Jack pulled a long straw from a bundle of hay and chewed on it. "You come over here the way Mr. Plummer told you, and we'll see. I'll try to think of something."

"All right."

"You say your pa and Old Harry agreed your mare was worth around ten dollars?"

"That's what they said."

Jack got up. "Well, you be here tomorrow. I'll put on my thinkin' cap."

18

David got up early on Sunday morning, although he and Grandpa had stayed up late watching the fireworks that were set off on Brown's Hill. He had given Grandpa Mr. Plummer's regards, but he hadn't told him anything about Lady's plight. He wasn't sure what he was going to have to do, and he didn't want Grandpa to stop him.

The men were setting up the jumps for the horse show when David got to the Myopia. A lot of people had brought wagons the night before and parked them next to the field, so they could watch in comfort.

One of the men whom David knew called to him to give a hand, so he tied Lady to a tree and went out to help with the jumps. The frames were set up and then the rails placed on them. A man in drill riding pants and shiny black boots went around measuring the jumps carefully.

When everything was set up, the men took David with them to eat breakfast at the big table set up on the grass near the stable. David, feeling ready to cave in from hunger, ate heartily of the pancakes and sausages. He wanted to talk to Jack, but whenever he saw him, Jack seemed to be too busy. David's spirits sank. Jack was his last hope. If he hadn't thought of anything, David would have to leave home, and he would have to do it today, before Papa came for Lady.

The crowd gathered, the wagons filling up with people and picnic baskets. Some of the contestants were riding their horses around the edge of the field. Most of the women rode sidesaddle, heavy riding skirts draped over their legs, but one young woman in a black velvet cap, white riding pants, and a green silk jacket, rode astride. As Grandpa had said last night, these people spent much of their lives on horseback, and you wouldn't find a better display of horsemanship anywhere in the world.

Children lined the border of the field, balancing on the thin white boards. Every now and then a man came by and warned them to keep back of the boards, but as soon as he left, they were on them again.

David looked nervously for Mr. Plummer and finally saw him sitting in a carriage with a young woman and four children. David prayed he wouldn't forget. It would surely be all right to take money from him this time, and David desperately needed some money if he were going away.

There was a stir of excitement as the first rider lined up by the first jump. Leaning forward and touching his horse lightly with his crop, he started suddenly, soaring beautifully over the first jump. He pulled the horse up, then urged him toward the second jump. There was no sound except the rider's low voice as he spoke to his horse, and the muffled pounding of the hooves on the grass. He came around the entire field, clearing every jump except the last one; a soft groan went up from the crowd as the horse's hooves clicked the top rail of the last jump. But it had been a fine demonstration, and David joined in the light flutter of handclaps.

For a while he watched the jumping intently, too engrossed in the grace and skill of the horses and their riders to think about anything else. But as the morning wore on, he began to worry. No sign of Jack, and David didn't want to bother him. David was sitting on Lady, to watch the show, and Jack could surely see him if he were looking for him.

He caught his breath as the shiny black horse that old Mrs. Barrett always rode stumbled and almost threw her at the third jump. She must be a million years old, he thought, but she's still one of the best riders here. She pulled up the horse's head and got him under control. Last year her youngest son had been thrown and killed, riding alone on their estate. She still wore a wide black mourning band on the arm of her riding coat.

If I went to Charlestown, to the navy yard, David thought, returning to his effort to plan something, I'd be in the city, and it would be hard to find a place for Lady. It would certainly cost more. Maybe New Hampshire or along the Maine coast would be better, someplace where they built boats. There was that man in Amesbury who built dories. . . . There was a navy yard at Portsmouth. . . . He wondered if he'd get lost. He'd been to Portsmouth once, and to Newburyport many times, both with Grandpa and with Papa, but he hadn't paid attention to the road. The thing to do would be to stick as close to the ocean as he could; that way he wouldn't get lost.

When the last of the morning jumpers had finished, David turned Lady's head toward the pavilion to wait for Mr. Plummer. He slid off Lady's back and paced up and down in the grass, tight as a spring, afraid Mr. Plummer wasn't going to remember.

But suddenly there he was, with the four children. "Good morning, David," he said. "Children, this is David O'Brien. These are my grandchildren, Nathaniel, Harrison, Amanda, and Emma."

The children said, "How do you do" politely, and David smiled with relief. "Good morning," he said. "I'm glad to know you."

Quite a few people had gathered at the pavilion to eat their lunch, and Mr. Plummer now turned toward them, raising his voice. "Ladies and gentlemen and especially children, David O'Brien here has a very talented little mare who used to work in the circus. He has kindly agreed to put her through her tricks. I'm sure he won't mind if you watch."

David flushed but he smiled at the people and said, "Not at all." He wished he could have done all this off by themselves, just the Plummers and Lady and him, but if this was the way Mr. Plummer wanted it, this was the way he'd do it.

He spoke to Lady, and almost before he finished the quiet command, she had pranced over to him, swinging one foreleg in front of the other as if she were dancing. He realized that the crowd that bothered him delighted her.

When the children cried out in pleasure she bobbed her head, and without waiting for David's command, she reared up and went around in a circle on her hind legs.

One of the children said, "Is it all right if we clap?"

"Oh yes. She likes it."

At the ripple of applause, she minced up to David and reared up, putting the front hooves very lightly on his shoulders. He lifted his arm high, and she backed away, still on her hind feet. He whistled a waltz tune and she danced. He leaped on her back and rode her around and around in a tight circle, standing up.

He saw out of the corner of his eye that the crowd had grown, and that Jack was there, watching him with a big grin. He began to enjoy himself as much as Lady seemed to be enjoying herself. He put her through every trick he could remember, and on her own she added a few more. The children were giggling and teetering on their toes with delight. They knew how to behave around horses, and none of them crowded her.

Finally, when he saw the riders who were going to ride in the afternoon events begin to gather out at the field, he wound up the show in a flourish. The children and many of their mothers came up to thank him and to gaze admiringly at Lady. Suddenly David saw Grandpa at the back of the crowd. He hadn't known he was coming to the show at all. He hoped he wouldn't disapprove of his putting Lady through her paces.

Mr. Plummer was talking to Jack. David thought he was not going to offer him any money this time—after all, they hadn't mentioned it—so he put his arm around Lady's neck and headed over toward Grandpa. But Mr. Plummer stopped him.

"David. I want to thank you. It was a lovely show. The

children were enchanted. We all were."

David, still a little out of breath, said, "It was fun."

Mr. Plummer held out his hand and offered a five-dollar gold piece to David. "You won't refuse me the pleasure of reimbursing you today for your time and trouble?"

"Thank you very much." The coin gleamed a dull yellow in David's hand.

Mr. Plummer held up his smallest granddaughter and let her stroke Lady's nose. "It is a pleasure to know you, David. And now I am going to say hello to your grandfather."

As Mr. Plummer and the children left, Jack came up to David. He was carrying a black derby hat. David looked at it in astonishment. It was full of money, bills and coins.

"It's yours, Davey."

"Mine? What do you mean?"

"Well, I thought to myself, if David is putting on a show for Mr. Plummer—and it was a very good show, Davey; you and Lady done yourselves proud—if Mr. Plummer and his little ones are watching Davey, I thought to myself, so will a lot of other people. Folks gather around here for lunch, you know, and they'd be watching. Well. . . ." He hesitated. "I just moved around through the crowd with my derby, in case they wanted to pay for their pleasure."

David was torn between shock and excitement. "Was that right? I mean, they could have watched it for nothing. . . ."

"Sure they could, you bet your life they could, and a lot of them did. But some wanted to let you know how much they enjoyed themselves."

"It makes me seem like a hurdy-gurdy player or something."

"Not a'-tall, Davey, not a'-tall. Nobody gave that didn't

want to, and you didn't ask for a penny. You didn't carry no tin cup with a monkey running around asking for money. You did it all out of your own good heart. Come on, let's go over to the stable and count it."

Bemused, David, leading Lady, followed Jack. Grandpa and Mr. Plummer had disappeared, gone out to the field, no doubt, to watch the afternoon jumping, which had already begun.

In the tack room that Jack used for his private office, he counted the money. "With the fiver Mr. Plummer gave you, you've got thirteen dollars and seventy-five cents."

David gasped. "Thirteen dollars!"

"And seventy-five cents." He smoothed out the bills and stacked the coins neatly. "Now Davey, it's none of my business, only you did tell me your troubles, and I got this to say. If I was you, I'd go see Old Harry myself, and I'd make him a proposition. I'd remind him he said your horse wasn't worth but six or seven dollars, but your papa said it was worth ten, so you'll offer him the ten."

David felt as if a weight had been lifted from his chest. "You mean he'd take the money instead of Lady?"

" 'Course he will. The kind of horse he uses, he can get for four or five dollars or even nothing, maybe just in a swap for sharpening up a few knives. Ten dollars to Old Harry is like a banquet to a starving man. The man's a miser. But Davey, one thing you got to be sure to do."

"What?"

"Be sure you get him to sign for it. If you don't, he'll swear on a stack of Bibles you never gave him nothing. You got to have an agreement all written out when you go to see him, or you'll lose your money and your horse, both."

"Have you got any paper?"

"You sit right here."

While Jack was gone, David kept counting the bills, sure there must be some mistake. But it was thirteen dollars and seventy-five cents, all right. He'd give Papa the three seventy-five toward whatever he'd need to fix the rig.

Jack brought back a sheet of Myopia Hunt Club stationery, and carefully cut off the name and the crest. "Now you write it out real careful, Davey."

David, who had won the penmanship prize in the eighth grade, put his tongue between his teeth and very carefully wrote out the agreement. "I, Harry. . . ." He looked at Jack. "What's his last name?"

"Don't know as he's got one. Say 'known as Old Harry the scissors grinder.' Ain't but one of them."

"I, Harry, known as Old Harry the scissors grinder, do hereby acknowledge receipt of ten dollars from David A. O'Brien, in full payment for the loss of my horse in an accident involving the automobile owned by Nathan O'Brien and others on the evening of June 29, 1910, in the town of Essex, county of Essex, Commonwealth of Massachusetts." David dipped the pen quill into the bottle of ink that Jack had brought, and carefully shook off the excess drops. "I hereby swear that I and all my heirs have no further claim whatsoever on aforesaid Nathan O'Brien in this matter. Signed: July 5, 1910." He read it to Jack.

"Davey!" Jack clapped him on the back. "You ought to be a lawyer. You got the gift."

"I've read all those old deeds and things that Grandpa has

collected." David was rather pleased with the document himself. He wished he had an official seal to stamp on it. "I better go right now," he said, "and if you see Grandpa, will you tell him I had to leave, but I'll see him soon."

"He don't know about all this?"

"No."

"I'll make a point of telling him what you said, so he won't worry." He scooped up the money and gave it to David. "And Davey, don't let Old Harry know you got any more than ten dollars. Keep the ten separate."

David distributed the money through his pockets. The coins made him feel heavy. "I'll leave Lady at Grandpa's and go home on my bike. Thanks an awful lot, Jack. You just about saved my life."

Jack shook hands with him. "You're a good lad. Good luck, now."

David ran out of the stable and got Lady. "Come on, girl. You've just been put out to pasture. You're a retired actress."

19

David left his bicycle out at the end of the path that led through the woods to Old Harry's cabin. Although it was a sunny day, the woods were dark, full of overgrown brush and scraggly bushes filling in the spaces between the trees. The path was narrow, uneven, and bumpy with the roots of trees. David stubbed his toe several times, and the last time nearly fell into a thick green clump of skunk cabbage.

In a few minutes he came within view of Old Harry's shack. It was a ramshackle little cabin that had been there at least since Papa was a little boy, because he remembered it. The roof was covered with tar paper, some of it torn, and there was a skinny stovepipe sticking up through it. A pile of rusted cans and old whiskey jugs and bottles leaned against one side. Newspapers were tacked up on the two windows to keep out the rain.

The broken rig was there, but David saw no sign of Old Harry. Perhaps he wasn't home. It was hard to believe anybody would stay in that shack any more than he had to.

David went up to the door and called. No one answered. He knocked on the rickety door, which was partly open, and called again. When there was still no answer, he gave the door a little shove with his foot, and then cautiously peeked in. There was no one in the shack. A pile of rags filled up one corner; a cot stood along a wall. There was a small, wood-burning stove, one kitchen chair, a small, scarred wooden table. The place smelled bad.

"Looking for somebody, Davey?"

David jumped. Old Harry had come up silently behind him, grinning his same grin that was half-humble, half-sly.

"I was looking for you." David tried to keep his voice steady. Harry had really startled him.

"What can I do for you, my boy?"

Although he had rehearsed it over and over, for a moment David couldn't think how to begin. He cleared his throat. "My father said he'd give you our old horse in place of yours that got killed. Will you take money instead?"

Old Harry's eyes were wary. "How much?"

"Ten dollars."

David saw the look of pleasure before Old Harry covered it up with hemming and hawing and rubbing his whiskery chin as if he had to think about it. "That ain't much money to replace a horse a man's had for fifteen years."

David knew he hadn't had that horse for fifteen years; no horse Old Harry had ever lasted that long; but he didn't argue. "You said our horse was worth six or seven dollars at the most. My father said she was worth ten, and you settled for that. I can give you the ten dollars."

"Let me see the money."

David hesitated, and for the first time he felt uneasy. Old Harry could take all his money and swear he'd never even seen David. Who would take a boy's word?

"I don't believe you got that kinda money."

David made himself calm down. He had to act grown-up, or Old Harry would think he could pull anything. "I've got it all right. But first I want you to sign an agreement."

Old Harry's eyes narrowed. "What agreement? What's that?"

David took it out of his pocket and read it to him.

"I can't read nor write."

"You can make an X. That's what people do when they can't write."

"There ain't no witnesses. How do I know it says what you say it says?"

"You'll have to take my word for it. I'm not a liar." For a second he felt like Papa, saying that.

Old Harry looked the agreement all over, right side up and upside down and on the back. "What you gonna do with it if I was to sign it?"

Although David hadn't thought of it till that moment, he said, "I'll give it to Mr. Milliken. He'll have it recorded."

Still Old Harry hesitated. "How do I know you ain't foolin' a poor old man like me?"

"I'm not fooling you." David took the ten dollars out of his pocket. He saw Old Harry's eyes gleam. "How could I be fooling you, when you can see the money?" He held it back as Harry reached for it. "Sign first."

"Ain't got no pencil."

David brought out the pencil Jack had given him and went inside to put the agreement on the table. He was sorry

as soon as he went into the shack. It smelled so bad, he thought he would gag. But this was no time to insult Old Harry. "Here, make an X right here." He held out the pencil. "What's your last name?"

"That's my business." The old man took the pencil, wet the lead between his colorless lips, and made a big scrawly X. "Now gimme the money."

David picked up the agreement and held out the gold piece, two ones, and the rest in change. He waited while the old man counted it. Old Harry bit the gold piece. "Your pa still has to fix that rig. He promised."

"He'll fix it. He keeps his word." David backed out of the shack and took a cautious breath of fresh air. He looked into the shack one last time and saw Old Harry counting the money, his hands shaking. David felt a sudden wave of pity. What a terrible way to live.

As soon as he was out of sight of the shack, he began to run. When he got to his bike, he rode like the wind until he came into his own yard. He wondered what Papa would say. He ought to be proud of him. Even Andrew never made all that money in that short a time.

Papa had the hood up on the Ford, peering helplessly into it. David felt nervous. If he could fix whatever was wrong with the machine, then Papa would be in a good mood to hear about Lady.

Papa looked up. He had a streak of grease on his face. "Goldarned thing won't perk right." He looked behind David. "Where's Lady?"

20

David peered down at the engine. “Maybe the gas line’s plugged.”

“I asked you where Lady is.”

“I was just going to tell you. She’s up at Grandpa’s, but. . . .”

Papa’s face flushed and he caught David by the shoulder. “I told you to get her back here today. Why did you disobey me?”

“Papa, I’m trying to tell you. I went to see Old Harry. I gave him money instead. He was glad to get it. Here’s the agreement he signed.”

Papa grabbed the piece of paper and read it. “Ten dollars! Where did you get hold of ten dollars? If you asked your grandfather. . . .”

“Grandpa doesn’t even know anything about it. It was my own money.”

Papa shook him. “Where’d you get ten dollars?”

David's own temper was rising. "Papa, if you'd give me a chance to tell you. . . ." He pulled away from his father's hand. "Why can't you ever give me a chance to say anything?"

His father folded his arms. "Tell it, then."

As briefly as he could, he told him about the two shows Lady had given, about Mr. Plummer, about Jack's derby full of money. "We earned the money fair and square. And there's three seventy-five left. You can use it to buy whatever you need to fix the rig." He held out the money.

"You begged for money, like a Gypsy."

David's voice rose. "I did not. Papa, will you cut it out and listen to what I'm telling you? I didn't even know Jack had that money. I didn't know about any money at all, except what Mr. Plummer offered me Saturday, and I refused that. I put on a show for them, and they liked it and they wanted to pay for it. It's no different than you getting paid for running people back and forth to the depot. It was a job. The only difference is, I would have done it for nothing, and you wouldn't take people to the depot for nothing."

"Don't sass me, David."

"I'm not. I'm telling you what happened. And now Old Harry is happy, and Lady will be all right."

Papa began to walk up and down, as if he could scarcely contain his anger. "You interfered in my business, without even telling me. I gave Old Harry my word. . . ."

"But he likes it this way. He got the good end of it."

"Lady is my horse. You act like she's yours."

David began to pace too, to keep up with Papa so he could talk to him. "She's one of the family. I've had her around almost all my life. You can't sell her the way you'd sell a bucketful of clams. She's almost like a person."

"She's a horse, damn it! A working animal. She's not any member of any damned human family."

"Did you *want* her to be beaten and starved?"

"I wouldn't have allowed her to be beaten and starved. You know that. I'm good to my animals."

"But she wouldn't have been yours any more. You couldn't have stopped Old Harry. He'd have ruined her in a month." David bit his lip.

"Who's going to pay for her keep? Your grandfather?"

"I'll get hay for her, just the way I always have."

"She'll need oats next winter."

"I'll get 'em."

His father wheeled around, glaring down at him. "You take an awful lot on yourself, David. Just because you work in the yard doesn't mean you're head of this family. You take it on yourself to handle my affairs, and I don't like it."

David lowered his voice. "Papa, if I hadn't got that money for Lady, I was going to take her and run away from home."

His father stared at him. "You were going to steal my horse?"

David's voice shook. "That's all it would mean to you, steal your horse. You wouldn't even care if I was gone."

His father looked away. "Well, you wouldn't have done it. You like to talk big."

"I was going to do it, and I can still do it."

His father looked up as Mama came into the yard, home from the concert at the town hall. His manner changed. "See if you can find out what's wrong with the Ford." He walked toward Mama.

His hands trembling, David got the old yardstick out of the automobile and stuck it in the gas tank. With real satisfaction he called to his father. "You let it run out of gas."

"Fill it up," his father said, and went into the house.

From then on, David made a point of checking the gas tank every morning, letting Papa see that he did it. Neither of them mentioned Lady again, nor did Mama. Papa brought Old Harry's rig in, hitched on to the back of his Ford, and repaired it until it was a whole lot better, David thought, than it had been before. If Papa talked to Old Harry about the money, he said nothing to David.

By mutual agreement, it seemed, Papa and David avoided each other, an avoidance made easier because both of them were especially busy. As Mr. Milliken and Uncle Tom had predicted, people began to call on Papa for all kinds of extra work with the Ford, sometimes a trip to Gloucester and Rockport for the summer people, sometimes moving small loads of almost anything from lobster crates to stacks of firewood, anything the owner wanted to move faster than a horse and wagon could do it. And he sold all the lobsters he could bring in.

The manager of the Oceanside Hotel in Magnolia made an arrangement with Papa to come once a week and take some of his guests on scenic drives around Gloucester Harbor to Eastern Point or up the shore to Manchester and Beverly Farms. At Mama's suggestion, Papa learned some of the history of the area so he could tell his passengers about it. David found it hard to imagine Papa giving his spiel, but the guests at the big rambling hotel, people from as far west as Cincinnati, seemed to like it better than sitting in their rocking chairs all day on the long veranda.

Papa still had troubles with the automobile. Once he ran it into a ditch, with a full load of ladies from the Oceanside, and had to be pulled out by a horse and team. Whenever he had engine trouble, he had no idea how to fix it, and he had to turn to David for help.

"For one thing you drive it too slow," David told him. "That's why you keep stalling and backfiring."

"If the Lord had meant for man to go more than fifteen miles an hour, he'd have given him wings," Papa said.

David held his tongue and went over the engine again. Following a tip he'd read in the paper, he put mothballs in the gas tank to give the engine pep. But Papa still stalled.

At the yard David and the others were working late every night, trying to get the *Minerva Four* ready for her launching date. David was allowed to do a lot more than run errands now. They even let him help a little with the finish work in the fo'c'sle and cabin. He would look at the trim little vessel sometimes and almost think of it as his own. "I drove those nails; I worked on that stretch of plank and helped make it lie fair." Sometimes at night, too tired even to talk to Mama, he would fall into bed and dream that it really was his vessel and he was going to sail it right around the world.

21

The night before the launching, David stayed with the men who were rushing to finish the last details. It had been decided that they would give the *Minerva Four* a side launching, instead of the conventional one. Instead of rigging a cradle for the vessel, they leaned her onto a single way, so she would skate into the water on her own keel and one bilge, entering the water almost on her beam ends. That way she would draw less water, and there would be less chance of the near-disaster they'd had with the *Mildred W*. It was a simpler and cheaper way to launch, and, as Pete said, "Flashier. We'll give 'em a good show."

The owner of the *Minerva Four* was driving down from Pride's Crossing with a party, and another group of his friends were coming by special train from Boston. Papa was to meet them at the depot. It would be the most important group of people to visit Essex in some time. There had been a rumor that President Taft himself might come, but later it was said he couldn't make it up from Washington to his

Pride's Crossing home.

Tonight David held a lantern while the men finished work on the ground way, which was built up under the turn of the bilge on one side. Underneath the keel and between the blockings that the boat was built on, they had arranged a series of greased wooden slabs. Big screw jacks leaned the boat onto the way. Tomorrow the carpenters would split away the supporting blocks and the keel would come to rest on the greased slabs. Then, when enough blocks were split out, she would move; she would be on her own.

David hated to see her go. He was planning to ride her down the river to Gloucester, just to make sure she got off all right, and to see how she felt in the water. Then he'd come home on the electric car.

"Ain't no other place in the country, so far as I know," Pete was saying, "that launches a vessel this way."

"Ain't no other place where they're good enough to do it," Horace said.

Pete looked up at the boat. "Well, Davey, we're going to miss her, ain't we."

"Yes," David said. "I wish I could stay with her."

"Maybe they'll need a cabin boy."

He smiled and shook his head. Some day he'd leave home, but not on a vessel and not just yet. For a second he thought about Lady. He hadn't seen her or Grandpa for a while; there had been so much to do lately, what with working so late at the yard, and trying to keep the Ford shipshape. Maybe this weekend he could go up and see them.

It was almost midnight when he got home. He noticed a light in Mrs. Pulsifer's living room, which surprised him, because she usually went to bed with the chickens. In his own house a lamp burned in the kitchen, and Mama had left him some supper on the back of the stove. Papa's hat was gone from the hook where it usually hung. Alarmed, he went out to see if the Ford was there. It was gone.

He ate absently, thinking about Papa. He hadn't been drinking much lately; surely he wouldn't pick tonight to go on a bender, not when he had to pick up those politicians at the train tomorrow. He didn't usually take the Ford out at night; he said he couldn't see to drive in the dark. And tonight would be really bad because there was a fog. David ate the chicken Mama had left him and tried to stop the nervous feeling in his stomach. He didn't think he could stand it if anything went wrong with the launching of the *Minerva,* and especially if it was Papa's fault. He wished Mama were awake so he could ask her where Papa was, but chances were she might not even know. Papa didn't like to account for his whereabouts, even to Mama.

When he got to bed, he tried to make himself go to sleep, but he had too many things on his mind. He hoped the side launch would work all right. There was an old shipyard superstition: don't launch on Friday. And tomorrow was Friday. He didn't think he was superstitious, but still it worried him.

The shreds of fog that drifted in his window made him feel cold. He pulled the quilt up around his neck. Finally, at least an hour after he had gone to bed, he heard the Ford come in the yard. It didn't sound right. One of the cylinders was missing, he thought. Well, the launching was at noon, and he didn't have to go to work in the morning, so he'd take a look at her. He heard Papa come in, and he sounded all right. David turned over and went to sleep.

22

David woke up at the regular time, remembered he didn't have to get up, and went to sleep again. It was the bonging of the clock downstairs that finally woke him again. He counted the strokes. Eleven! He couldn't believe it! He rolled out of bed and began to dress in a hurry. Why hadn't Mama called him?

Another sound caught his attention. Rain. It was pouring. He closed the window as the rain drummed against it. Looked like a thunderstorm. Funny Mama hadn't come up to close the window, at least. The launching was at twelve. The train was due in at quarter of. He had intended to work on that missing cylinder, but now there wouldn't be time.

Calm down, he told himself; cool off. There's time at least to look at it. At least half an hour before Papa leaves for the depot. He ran downstairs, buttoning his shirt as he went. There was no one around. He looked in the sitting room, called upstairs, but the house was empty. Then he saw the note from Mama on the table. "Hope you had a good sleep, dear. You needed it. I'm looking after some things for Mrs. P. If I don't get back in time for the launching, give the *Minerva* my blessing. Breakfast on back of stove. Love, Mama."

He was disappointed. He particularly wanted Mama to see the *Minerva* go into the river. His boat. What was so pressing about Mrs. P.? He assumed she meant Mrs. Pulsifer, next door. Maybe she was sick; her light had been on last night. Still standing up, he ate the fried ham and the hash-browned potatoes and drank some milk, anxiously watching the storm. It looked like a shower. Already there was a lifting of clouds in the west. He pulled on his oilskin coat and ran out to the barn to take a look at the auto. Maybe Papa was out here. He ought to be around somewhere; it was getting near time.

But he wasn't in the barn. David felt exasperated. In spite of the extra sleep, he still felt the fatigue of all those long days in the yard, and especially the late work last night. He was proud that they'd got the *Minerva* ready on time, but it had cost a lot in energy. Because of the storm, the barn was even darker than usual. He came around the driver's side of the automobile just as a flash of lightning streaked across the high, dusty barn window. He gasped.

The whole side of the auto was caked with mud and deeply scratched, and the front left fender was crumpled up like a piece of pleated cloth. For a minute he just leaned against the door, stunned. What could have happened? Papa had had it out last night. *Why?* He *knew* he wasn't a good enough driver to go out at night. He must have wanted to show it off to somebody. Then smashed it up on the way home. He couldn't have been hurt, or Mama would have said so. Maybe he got drunk and drove it into a ditch. No, he didn't even need to get drunk to drive it into a ditch; he could do it cold sober. Furiously, David punched the seat with his fist. Of all times to have a wreck! Why couldn't Papa ever be depended on?

Well, he had half an hour to clean it up and get it going. He grabbed a pail and filled it at the pump, and scrubbed off as much of the mud and dirt as he could. The finish was really scarred up. He tried to straighten the fender but he couldn't. He did bend it back so it wasn't pressing against the tire. Lucky Papa didn't have a flat tire, the way the metal was scraping against it.

He looked for the crank, praying the car would run. From the outside, at least, it didn't look as if the engine itself had been damaged. He felt around in the dark for the crank. It wasn't under the seat, where Papa kept it. He ran his hand all around the floor, trying to find the crank, but it wasn't there. He looked in back. Not there. He was beginning to feel panicky. What could have become of it? Where was Papa? Maybe he *had* been hurt.

He came out of the barn and saw Papa coming into the yard. He was soaking wet, and he limped a little. As he came closer, David saw he had a black eye and a deep scratch on his cheek.

"Papa! What happened? Did you get hurt?"

"No. I'm all right." His father looked distracted.

"Did you tip over or what?"

"She fell on her side in a ditch. Nothing serious."

"Nothing serious! How did you happen to be out at night? You know you can't drive at night. Where were you?"

Papa looked a little bewildered. "I was. . . . I was coming

back the Beverly road. . . ."

David interrupted him. "The Beverly road!" Once he and Andrew had had to take the buggy and go bring Papa home, drunk, from a saloon just over the Beverly line. "You went to that saloon. You got drunk and wrecked the car."

Papa looked at him with a frown, as if he wasn't sure he had heard him correctly. "What?"

Thunder crashed, and the rain poured down in a last torrent as the sky began to clear.

"How could you do it, when you've got to meet those people?"

"You don't seem to be up on the news," Papa said.

David was too upset to be cautious. "What news? What's happened to the crank? What did you do with the crank?"

"I lost it. I've been out looking for it."

David couldn't believe it. "You lost it!"

"It may have fallen off the running board. I may have laid it down after I cranked her up, in the ditch."

"How do you expect me to start the auto without the crank?"

Suddenly Papa's temper exploded. "I don't expect you to start it. So far as I know, it hasn't got a damned thing to do with you. Now if you'll get out of the way, I'll try to get it going." He strode into the barn and began to push on the front of the car.

David followed him in, leaned into the automobile, and released the brake. His father gave him a furious look. David leaned on the other fender and the auto slowly rolled backward out into the yard.

"I don't need your help," Papa said. His face looked distorted, with the swelling around the blackened eye. The flesh was purple and green. David suddenly felt sorry for him.

"Papa, I'm sorry you got hurt. Let me help you get the machine going."

"I don't need your help, and I don't need your sympathy." He took his watch out of his pocket and looked at it. "Well, get in, and I'll push it down the yard. Maybe she'll start."

David climbed into the seat, but he felt more like going off and leaving Papa to cope with it. You tell him you're sorry, and he snarls at you. If it weren't so important to get those people to the launching, David thought, he wouldn't even try to get the auto going.

Papa pushed and pushed, but there wasn't enough of an incline to make the engine start. Panting for breath, he leaned against the side of the automobile. "No use. I'll have to get a carriage at the livery stable."

"You won't get there in time."

Raising his voice, Papa said, "Then they can damned well wait for me." He strode off down the yard to the street without looking back.

The rain stopped abruptly. David put up the hood and began to fiddle. There must be *something* he could do. He waved absently as Pinky and Joey Fuller rode their bikes past the yard. Then, on second thought, he ran out to the street and called them back.

"Listen, I've got to get this thing going. The crank got lost. If you push me just as hard as you can, get me going fast as you can till I hit that little downslope in front of Pulsifers, I think she'll go."

"Won't go without no crank," Joey said.

"Try it," David said impatiently. "Listen, if you get me going, I'll take you for a ride later. Honest."

The boys started to push. David leaned out. "Faster!"

The Ford began to move. They got it out to the street, and David turned it into the right direction. Now if they could just get him up over the little hump before the Pulsifer place, then he'd have a good downgrade. "Push!" he yelled. "Got to get it going lickety-split."

"Whaddaya think we are, draft horses?" Pinky yelled back. But they pushed, and the Ford moved up the slope to the top of the grade.

"Now! Big shove! Hard as you can do 'er."

He felt the Ford begin to pick up speed. He didn't know whether the boys were still pushing or not. Frantically he advanced the spark a little further, fiddled with the throttle, held the foot clutch in high gear. Nothing happened. He was almost at the bottom of the grade, where the street leveled out again. It was now or never.

Suddenly it caught. He moved the throttle up a little more, careful not to stall. It was running! With a wild wave of his arm to thank the boys, he drove down the street. Terrified of stalling, he drove faster than Papa ever did. He saw the men at the blacksmith shop turn to look as he went by, but he didn't dare take his hand off the wheel to wave. The road was wet and full of deep puddles, but he splashed through them without slowing down.

Just before he got to the livery stable, he passed Papa, walking fast, almost stumbling with his limping leg. David shouted, but he knew Papa couldn't hear him above the engine. He didn't dare to stop. Just as he passed Papa, he hit a mud puddle. Horrified, he saw Papa splashed with muddy water. He gave a quick wave with his left arm, hoping Papa would see it and understand he was sorry, but he had to grab the wheel with both hands again as he hit a hole in the road.

"Papa, I didn't mean to splash you," he said aloud. But why did Papa do everything wrong? How could he expect to go rampaging around at night and have everything run smooth as clockwork the next day? How could he take such a chance the night before the launching? He must know how much this vessel meant to David. But maybe he didn't. It was hard to know what Papa knew or thought because he so seldom told you.

When David got to the depot, the train had just come in. There was just one car, a parlor car, and the engine-and-coal car. Black smoke funneled up from the smokestack on the engine. Four men and two women got out of the parlor car, helped down by Tom Blake, the brakeman, and Harris Peters, the conductor. Harris pointed out David and the taxi, and the people from Boston laughed. One of them strolled over to David. He was wearing a black raincoat.

"What is that thing, son?"

"It's two Fords put together, sir. It makes a good taxi."

"That's quite an idea. Did your father do that?"

"No. We got it from some man who likes to fool with machines."

The others came up, and the men helped the ladies into the taxi. David had left the engine running, and he was praying it wouldn't stall. He climbed into the driver's seat and advanced the throttle a little.

"Can you drive this creation?" one of the ladies asked him. "You look too young."

"Yes, ma'am, I can drive it. I drive it all the time."

"Are you the regular taximan? Don't you go to school?"

"Yes, I go to school. My father is the regular taximan."

"Children don't go to school in summer, Adelaide," the other woman said. They all laughed, as if she had said something very funny.

"I hope it doesn't rain again," one of the men said. "I don't relish the thought of standing out in the rain to watch Mortimer's stupid boat slide into the briny."

Stupid boat. David bit his lip. He turned the Ford around, trying to avoid the worst of the puddles, but he heard one of the women squeal as water splashed up on the side. He concentrated so fiercely on driving at a speed that would prevent stalling, still trying to avoid the worst bumps, that his fingers ached from clutching the steering wheel.

"Your machine is missing on one cylinder," the man who sat next to him said.

"I just noticed that this morning," David said. "Didn't have time to get it looked at."

"Who takes care of your auto for you, down here in the sticks?"

"I do it myself."

"Smart youngster," the man said. "What's your name?"

"David O'Brien."

The man half-turned around. "Our driver is David O'Brien. Not only drives this thing, but is his own mechanic."

"The man of the future," one of the other men said.

"How can you ever do it by yourself?" the younger of the women asked. "How did you know how?"

"Well, there's a diagram that comes with it." David wished they wouldn't talk to him. He wanted to give the driving his whole attention.

"That's Ford's boast," the man in the black raincoat said. "The Ford is a machine any man with a screwdriver and a piece of baling wire can keep running."

One of the women clutched the side post as they hit a hole. "This town needs some new roads."

"Well, you're in the country now, Adelaide," the man in the raincoat said. "This isn't Beacon Street."

David watched out for Papa, thinking he might see him near the livery stable, but there was no sign of him.

He didn't see him again until the *Minerva Four* was ready to be launched. Then he caught sight of him, taking pictures of the vessel and the crowd, just as if nothing had happened.

The woman named Adelaide swung the bottle of champagne as the *Minerva Four* gave a loud creak and a groan and started down the greased slabs toward the water. The men standing near her jumped clear, David with them. The crowd cheered, the tug hooted. David was standing close to the water's edge. He caught a glimpse of Papa moving in to get another picture.

Somebody yelled, and almost at the same moment there was a high, whistling noise. David heard Pete yell, "Hawser's splitting!" He just had time to glance up at the big hawser that was attached to the drag. It was coming apart in the middle. Before David could move, the two ends separated and one end of the thick rope snaked through the air with ferocious speed. It hit David in the side of the head and knocked him into the water.

23

David tried to open his eyes, but he couldn't do it. A sharp pain seemed to crack right through his skull. He didn't know where he was or what had happened. Because it was too much effort trying to move or open his eyes, he lay still. He could hear voices close to him.

"God, that hit him an awful wallop." It was Horace's voice, without the usual cheer in it.

Pete's voice answered. "I never saw that happen before."

"Nathan dove into that river so fast, you could hardly see but a streak."

Another voice said, "Is he going to be all right?"

"His father's gone for the doctor."

"I saw him running down the street like all hell was after him. Soaking wet, coat flapping. Looked a sight."

"Nathan sets great store by them boys of his."

"Ought to get a coat under the boy's head."

"No, don't touch him till the doc comes."

Far off, David heard the toot of the towboat's whistle.

"Got a good launch, other than the boy getting hurt."

"Good launch."

David felt himself drifting away from their voices. When he could hear them again, someone was saying, "Where's the kid's ma?"

"She's with Minnie Pulsifer. She don't know about Davey."

The voice of one of the dubbers said, "Where'd Nathan git that shiner? He git in a fight or something?"

"No," Pete Alzar said. "He drove Mrs. Pulsifer up to Beverly to the hospital. She was took with appendicitis in the middle of the night. Doc operated at the house, but she was sinkin', so they got her to the hospital."

"It don't give a man a shiner to go up to Beverly," the dubber said.

"Well, it was foggy. On the way home he ran off into the ditch."

Horace said, "Doc said it was lucky Nathan was around with his auto. Minnie might not have made it. She was took real bad."

David tried to make sense out of what he was hearing. It was hard to remember anything. He tried once more to open his eyes.

"Kid's eyelids is flutterin'."

"He'll be all right. Got a concussion, most likely."

"What the hell do you know, Archie?" Horace sounded annoyed.

Then David heard his father's voice, tight with anxiety, and the answering voice of the doctor. He felt fingers on his pulse, and then he felt himself very gently lifted up. He stopped trying to make sense of anything.

For a period of time that he was unable to keep any track of, David lay in his bed. Sometimes he opened his eyes to find his mother there, or the doctor, or his father. Often he woke to find one of his parents sitting in the rocking chair that they'd brought up from downstairs. From time to time his mother tried gently to get him to eat, and after a while he was able to eat a little soup and drink a little milk. His head was bandaged, and it ached. He felt dizzy whenever he tried to lift his head, but most of all he was worried, and he couldn't remember what he was worried about.

Every time the doctor came, he asked the same questions: How did he feel? Did he have pain? Was one side feeling weaker than the other? Finally David heard him say, "I think he's going to be all right, Mrs. O'Brien. I don't see any signs of fracture. But we'll keep him quiet for a while."

"When can I go to work?" David felt immensely relieved at being able to put the nagging worry into words. It was that, then, that had been worrying him.

"We'll see, Davey. You just take good care of yourself and do what your mother says. You're coming along fine."

One of the times when he opened his eyes to find his mother in the rocking chair mending clothes, he said, "Did the *Minerva* get off all right?"

"Oh, just fine, dear. I didn't see her, I'm sorry to say; I was up at the hospital with Mrs. Pulsifer. But everyone said she launched beautifully. A lovely boat."

Mrs. Pulsifer. That had been nagging at the back of his mind too, and he remembered now what he had heard the men say. "Is Mrs. Pulsifer getting better?"

His mother smiled and nodded. "She's coming alone fine. She had her appendix out, you know. It all happened so fast, I guess nobody really told you. It's just a good thing Papa had the taxi, because her appendix had ruptured and she would probably have died."

That was it. Papa had taken Mrs. Pulsifer to the hospital and then he'd had a wreck coming home in the fog, and David had thought he was drunk or just carousing around. He closed his eyes. A little later he heard Mama say softly, "I think he's asleep."

And Papa said, "I'll stay a while."

He heard the creak of the rocker as Papa sat down, and Mama's light steps going down the stairs. Pretty soon he could hear the piano, the sound muffled. Mama was giving a lesson, and she must have closed the doors to keep it from bothering him. He opened his eyes.

"Papa."

His father had his reading glasses on, reading the paper. One of the lenses was cracked, so he often closed that eye when he read. He looked over the tops of the glasses now, the way Grandpa did. "How are you feeling, son?"

"Better. Not so dizzy."

"Good." He folded the paper into a small square. "Feel up to looking at a picture?" He handed it to David. It was the *Salem Evening News*. David tried to lift his head to see better. Papa pushed the pillow under his head to make a little higher headrest.

David looked at the picture in the square Papa had folded. "It's the *Minerva*," David said. "The *Minerva* on her way down to the river." The picture had caught the vessel just as her stern hit the water, the spray flying up around her. "That's a dandy picture. Did you take it?"

Papa nodded, looking pleased. "Snapped it just before the hawser broke."

"Gee, that's great. Did the *News* pay you?"

"Yep. Five dollars."

David leaned back, looking at his father. "That's fine." He felt weak, but he wanted to talk to his father. "Papa, thank you for saving my life."

His father smiled. "If I hadn't been there, somebody else would have fished you out."

"I'm glad it was you." He waited a minute. "Papa, I didn't mean to splash mud all over you, when I was going to the depot. . . ."

"Never thought you did, son."

"I felt bad about it. See, I couldn't slow down without stalling."

"You did fine, getting it going and getting the people here. You did fine." His father picked up the paper and put it on his knees, but he took off his glasses.

David was trying to think straight, and it made his head hurt. "I wasn't very nice to you. See, I didn't know about Mrs. Pulsifer, and I thought. . . ."

"I know what you thought," Papa said quietly.

"I shouldn't have jumped to conclusions like that. It wasn't fair."

"Well, I'd say you had reason a-plenty to come to that particular conclusion. I'm not always what you'd call a dependable man."

David glanced sideways at his father's face. "You were

the one, though, that they depended on to get Mrs. Pulsifer to the hospital."

Papa shrugged. "I was the one with the auto."

David's head ached, partly because he wanted so much to talk, and it was such an effort. He was thinking of the time Andrew broke his ankle at the ice pond, and Papa carried him home all that way in his arms. And the way the old men sitting around the stove up at the store would say, "Davey, ask your pa to pick me up a bottle of Sloan's liniment when he goes by the drugstore, will you?" And the way on cold winter mornings Papa would stop on his way to the depot and give the little kids a ride to school. And he was always the one who kept an eye on Old Man Jasper, when he was drinking hard and sometimes passing out right on the street; Papa would take him home every time. Why hadn't he ever noticed these things before?

He had to speak, headache or no headache. "Papa, there's a lot that kids don't know, even when they think they know it all. Andrew used to say I was a smart aleck, and he was right."

"Oh, don't run yourself down, boy," Papa said.

"Well, I worried too much. I thought we might end up in the Poor Farm or something."

Papa was silent for a moment. "Well," he said, still not looking at David, "the more you go through, the more you kind of see that it isn't as easy as you might think to do the right thing all the time. Or even know what it is. Not that that excuses a man for not doing the right thing. I just say it isn't easy. But I think we'll steer clear of the Poor Farm, all right."

"I think an awful lot of you, Papa."

His father turned his head and looked at him, with the rare smile that lit up his somber face. "I'm glad to hear that, Davey." Then he changed his tone. "You got all kinds of people that think a lot of you. Do you know what's downstairs?"

"No. What?"

"Money. Your money."

David was puzzled. "You mean my pay from the yard?"

"More than that. The fellows at the yard took up a collection for you. More than thirty dollars down there in the sugar bowl, all yours."

David could hardly believe it. "Why'd they do that?"

"They like you. You worked hard, as good as any man, they told me. And another thing: one of those men you brought from the station, the one says he talked to you about the Ford. . . ."

"Yes, I remember him."

"Wrote me a letter telling me what a fine boy you are: bright boy, he says; and he and his friends were sorry you got hurt, and he sent you a check for twenty-five dollars."

David stared at the ceiling. "Gosh," he said finally.

"So don't worry about missing time at the yard. You'd never have made this much." He chuckled. "Not that I recommend getting your head cracked open as a means of income."

"That's wonderful." David could hardly take it in. "All that money. People are nice. Well, Mama can have most of it, same as if I'd earned it at the yard."

"No, we're going to put it in the bank account."

"What bank account?"

"Why, the one we're saving in for your college education."

"I didn't know you were."

"Well, there isn't much in there. But whenever we can, we put away a few dollars. There probably won't be enough, and you'll have to help work your way through. . . ."

It was the first time the idea of college had had any reality for David. "Papa! I could do that easy!" A pain shot through his head, and he winced.

"Take it easy, boy. The doctor said you weren't to get nerved up. Just take it easy."

"I'm all right."

"You rest a while now."

David fell asleep. It was dusk when he woke up, and Mama was standing there with a bowl of clam chowder. "Did your father tell you about his job?" she said, helping him to sit up.

"What job?"

"Harvey Milliken worked it out some way so your father is going to deliver the mail."

"That's wonderful!"

"Well, old Wilbur Jones wanted to retire, and Harvey heard about it. He pulled a few strings, I imagine. But having the Ford is what really won the day. Papa can deliver the mail in half the time it took Wilbur and his horse."

"We're rich, Mama."

She laughed. "Not quite. But it will be very good for your father. And a steady income. Here, try to eat it all, dear. Your grandfather wants you to come visit him for a week as soon as you feel up to it."

"A week? I've got to get back to work."

She shook her head. "The doctor says not yet. Working so hard in that hot sun wouldn't be good for you."

David felt too languid to worry. So much good news. He finished off the chowder. "When can I get up?"

"Tomorrow, for part of the day."

David lay back, thinking. "It's funny. I feel about ten years older."

She kissed him on the forehead, below the bandage. "I wouldn't want you to age that fast. Get some sleep now, dear."

But he lay awake a long time, thinking about all the things that had happened. He could hear Mama rattling the dishes, and Papa shaking down the stove. Then after a while he heard Mama playing the piano, playing the Grieg concerto that she'd played in her recital when she graduated from the conservatory. David liked it. But somewhere during the *Andante,* he fell asleep.

24

Grandpa had come for him with Pegasus and the little buggy, and when Mama said, "Father, we could have driven him to Hamilton and saved you the trip," Grandpa had answered, "I didn't want the boy joggled to death in any damned machine."

Mama had laughed and hugged him and talked him into staying for dinner. Papa was out on the mail route, so the three of them ate alone. The bandage was off David's head; he had just a big square of gauze held on with adhesive tape, over the cut the hawser had made. He still felt weak and sometimes a little dizzy, but the pains in his head were very infrequent now, and he didn't worry so much about everything.

As Pegasus trotted along with his elegant gait, David said, "How's Lady?"

"Oh, she's all right. I think we got her out to pasture just in time, though. Her other leg's stiffening up some now."

David frowned. "You don't think I hurt her any, putting on that show?"

"No, no. Not a bit. And from all I hear, she enjoyed it as much as anybody. Doc Crane said he never saw a horse having such a good time."

"I should have come up to see her before this. But we were working long hours on the *Minerva*."

Grandpa nodded. "She never noticed."

David felt a little hurt. "She probably missed me though. She's used to having me around."

Grandpa looked at him. "Davey, a horse doesn't miss people. Sometimes a dog does, though I suspect not as much as people like to think. But with a horse, it's out of sight, out of mind."

"But she loves me. She's . . . we spent years together." He felt distressed.

"She loves you when you're there. She's not going to eat her heart out when you're not." He glanced at David. "Am I upsetting you? You're not to be upset, I'm told."

"No, of course not," David said, but he *was* upset.

"The way a horse reacts to love is probably a good object lesson for man."

"What do you mean?"

"Well, when it's there, it's fine. When it isn't, forget about it. Find something else to love."

David thought that sounded cynical, but he said nothing. Cynical and not even true, because look how Grandpa grieved over Grandma.

"Love is only useful when it's in working condition." Grandpa flicked the whip over Pegasus's ear to drive off a greenhead fly. "Damned flies are something wicked this year."

The little horse switched his glossy tail over his back.

"Did you hear about Papa's job?"

"Yes. Your mother told me."

"Isn't it great?"

Grandpa didn't answer for a moment. "I guess it is. I'm sure it will make him happier, bringing in a steady income and all that. Sometimes, though, it seems sad to me that a man has to base his happiness on a steady income."

David thought about that, but he didn't know what Grandpa meant.

"Your father's become a victim of the machine age, and I'm sorry it had to happen to him. He should have been allowed to develop his life in his own way."

"Did you see his picture in the *Salem News?*"

"Yes. That's part of what I mean. Nathan might have been a good photographer; he has a good eye. But he came to it too late. Time is so often the villain." He looked at David. "What are you going to do when you're out of school?"

Ever since Papa told him about the bank account, David had been thinking about this. "I think I'd like to be a newspaperman, like you."

Grandpa looked pleased but he said, "Well, hold on now. It's not all adventure, you know. There's a lot of bone-breaking hard work and monotony."

"That's what I want to do, though."

"It isn't just a roomful of mementos."

"I know that. I've thought about it."

Grandpa drove in silence for a while. "Well, I'll help you all I can, if you're still of the same mind when the time comes." Then he added, "If I'm still around."

David's fingers touched the little silver thimble box in his pocket that held the tip of the bayonet. "Grandpa, why did you give me the Crazy Horse bayonet tip that day? You weren't feeling sick or anything, were you?"

Grandpa laughed. "No. It wasn't in the nature of a bequest. Let's see, why did I?" He pushed his Panama hat back on his head and mopped his damp forehead. "Something about your father. We'd been talking about your father. I think I got a notion about men who are born too late. Crazy Horse would have been a great chief, but he came too late."

David didn't quite see. "What about Papa?"

"Let's see, what was it I had in mind. . . ."

"If you think he'd have been a great photographer, he couldn't have been born too much earlier or the camera wouldn't have been invented."

Grandpa didn't seem to have heard him. As they went over the little bridge to his house, he said,

" '*Miniver scorned the gold he sought,*
But sore annoyed was he without it;
Miniver thought, and thought, and thought,
And thought about it.

Miniver Cheevy, born too late,
Scratched his head and kept on thinking;
Miniver coughed, and called it fate,
And kept on drinking.' "

When they reached the barn, he said, "Well, well, many of us have a bit of Miniver in us. There's your horse, Davey."

David slid out of the buggy and went down to the meadow to see Lady. He wanted to run and run, and throw his arms around her, but he wasn't that steady on his feet yet. He called to her, and she turned her head to look at him. He whistled, and she ambled toward him. He saw that she did indeed walk stiffly on her front legs. He threw his arms around her neck.

"Good Lady. Good old girl. I'm sorry I was away so long." No matter what Grandpa had said, he knew she'd missed him. "I won't stay away so long again." He rubbed the soft velvet of her nose. "Don't you worry, Lady. Everything's going to be just fine. Just fine."

She nickered softly and snuffed in his ear.